Chuck Jerman

BLACKIE SULLIVAN

Inspired by a true story

Archway Publishing books may be ordered
through booksellers or by contacting:

Archway Publishing
1663 Liberty Drive
Bloomington, IN 47403
www.archwaypublishing.com
1 (888) 242-5904

Because of the dynamic nature of the Internet, any web
addresses or links contained in this book may have changed
since publication and may no longer be valid. The views
expressed in this work are solely those of the author and do
not necessarily reflect the views of the publisher, and the
publisher hereby disclaims any responsibility for them.

Any people depicted in stock imagery provided by Thinkstock are
models, and such images are being used for illustrative purposes only.
Certain stock imagery © Thinkstock.

ISBN: 978-1-4808-4761-3 (sc)
ISBN: 978-1-4808-4759-0 (hc)
ISBN: 978-1-4808-4760-6 (e)

Library of Congress Control Number: 2017910125

Print information available on the last page.

Archway Publishing rev. date: 07/03/2017

IN MEMORY OF
John E. Sullivan (1928-2008) who shared with me
this story of his Grandfather, Blackie Sullivan.

DEDICATION
This book is dedicated to my wife, Judy
Jerman, who encouraged me and helped
me to put this story onto paper.

I

Blackie Sullivan was always running. Anytime anyone saw the young Cayuse man with the tan skin and the shock of black hair, he was mid-stride. His arms and legs pumped in perfect timing with each other. They were like a locomotive had come to life as a young man. The pistons he was graced with could put a steam engine to shame for their timing and precision. He wasn't running for the joy of it -- though he did enjoy it immensely. He was running because the summer in Washington State could quickly climb above eighty degrees and ice melted pretty quickly in the eighty degree heat.

Blackie worked for the SP&S railroad, loading and unloading the ice. He was responsible for packing the produce cars, which was usually considered the hardest job in the business. The blocks of ice could weigh over a hundred pounds. On some days, Blackie was pretty sure the blocks weighed more than he did. As they were sweating into his back, chilling his spine to the bone, he imagined he could actually feel them getting lighter. The work curved his back and rubbed his shoulders raw. At the end of every day, his knees were swollen and angry, thrumming with the beat of his heart. His lungs burned, and his hips screamed. The work was the kind of thing the people of Washington expected of Native Americans. Not content with just the conquest and plunder of his ancestral home, the white folks who had moved into Cayuse land demanded that Natives do the work they didn't want to do. That's what brought Blackie to Walla Walla every morning. Every morning, he strapped the heavy blocks of ice onto his back and set off on his rounds. He delivered the ice to the different taverns, markets, and hotels around town. Anyone that needed ice could expect a visit from a sweat-soaked Blackie Sullivan at some point during the day. They paid for the ice by weight, though, which meant that the longer Blackie took to deliver it, the less it weighed. If the ice melted too much, SP&S wouldn't even turn a profit. The young Cayuse felt a strange kind of loyalty to SP&S. Growing up as the last son of a conquered people, he'd faced every kind of indignity in his childhood. The brothers who ran SP&S were pretty good to him, all things considered. Even more than that, though, he took pride in what he did.

Walla Walla was a ramshackle frontier town that depended on him to keep it refrigerated. Without him, the lettuce would wilt and turn to mush, the meat would spoil and turn rancid. The white folks of Walla Walla might have thought he was a second-class citizen, but they depended on him to keep them fed. He took pride in that.

So, Blackie devoted himself to doing his job as best he could. He hoisted the blocks of ice up onto his back, tightened down the leather straps that held it to his back, and set off every morning. Each morning started with the slowest delivery of the day. He had to get his legs stretched out and his limbs warmed up. By the heat of the day, when the sun was literally melting away the profits, he was in his finest form. That's when the farmers, merchants, and railroad workers would meet at a tavern called the Look-See for an afternoon beer before heading back out to their respective jobs. The bar was a clapboard thing thrown together from the wood of the original wagons and train cars that had brought white conquerors into what came to be known as Washington Territory. The mismatched wood was slathered with globby white paint to keep it from decaying in the windswept town. The gaping holes and splinters did nothing to keep the heat out of the bar, though. The patrons were frequently stomping through ankle-deep dust as they swilled steam beer. Unlike the crisp, clear beer of the well-coiffed and feminized east coasters, the bearded and callused men of Washington drank steam beer from heavy metal steins.

Steam beer was brewed by different alehouses and breweries up and down the Pacific Coast. They didn't have the ice or the refrigeration needed to keep the brewing beer as cold as lager yeast demanded, so instead of the cold-brewed and clean-tasting lager of the advanced cities, this beer was a harsh and warm-brewed lager that had only the wind off the near-by Blue Mountains to cool it during the brewing process. Outside of Washington, no one probably would subject themselves to the strong flavors of steam beer, but here, they thought it was a sign of their independence. They didn't need New York City or Chicago to get a buzz on while at work.

That's what brought the railroad workers and farmers into the Look-See at the heat of the day. The sun was at its highest point. They'd been suffering through the long consecutive days of high heat and no rain. The floor of the Look-See was dry as old bones and stirred to dust with the slightest breeze. A farmer known only as Buddy put his dusty boots up on the empty chair at his table. He took a long draught of his foamy steam beer, leaving white head in his mustache. He sucked his mustache clean with his bottom lip.

The other man at the table was a small man named King Roger. He was a thin man who worked for the railroad. He was small in practically every way except his ego and his shoulders. Swinging a 12 pound sledgehammer for the railroad had turned his shoulders into boulders and his chest into slabs of rock. His ego he was born with. They called him King Roger because he claimed that he was related to the English monarchy. Whenever you asked him, though, his story changed. He would give someone a detailed lineage all the way from his mom back to one of the English kings. One day, it would be King George III, the king who lost the American colonies. The next day, he would be descended from King James. A few times, he even slipped up and said he was descended from King Louis XVI. Someone pointed out that Louis was French, not English; that just started a fight.

On this day, he was sitting with Buddy at a bar, staring out the open window of the Look-See. King Roger checked the clock on the wall. It was historically unreliable, but it was probably pretty close.

King Roger took a long sip. "Blackie should be round 'fore long."

Buddy nodded. "Same bet?"

King Roger nodded.

Buddy fished a crumpled, oily dollar bill out of his overalls. He tossed it on the table; the dollar slowly un-crumpled itself. King Roger eyed it while sipping his beer.

King Roger cleared his throat and said, "My money isn't exactly, uh, liquid at the moment. I reckon I'll have to take this one on credit."

Buddy scoffed. "You ain't paid me the last two times you lost."

Roger hit his stein against the table. "All the more reason to gimme a chance to win my money back."

Buddy was about to open his mouth to protest how stupid of a deal that would be for him, but Roger pointed his metal beer stein out the window.

"Here he comes," Buddy hollered.

They both jumped to their feet and stumbled to the window. Across the dusty dirt road in front of the Look-See, Blackie Sullivan raced into view. He was shirtless, sweat and melting ice glistening on his tan skin. He was wearing a loose pair of breeches tied up at the ankle so they didn't flap when he ran. He was barefoot, his feet slapping in the dirt and calling up little dust clouds with every footfall. He was moving so fast, his feet were perpetually obscured by a cloud of dust. The massive, sweating block of ice wept on his back.

His silky black hair flapping in the wind, he crossed in front of the Apothecary. Buddy and Roger both looked at the clock on the wall. The second hand had just passed the 10. They looked back out onto the street.

Blackie Sullivan sprinted through the street dragging dust behind himself like a comet's tail. He passed in front of the hotel. Buddy checked the clock again. Seventeen seconds had passed. Buddy bit his lip. They were betting on how long it would take Blackie Sullivan to get from the Apothecary to the Green Tavern. The bet was typically the same thing: one minute. Buddy usually picked the under, and Roger picked the over. If Blackie Sullivan made it from the Apothecary to the Green Tavern in under a minute, Buddy would win a dollar. If he took longer than one minute, Roger would win. Blackie almost always made it in under one minute, but today, he looked like he was slacking. It could have been the heat or the humidity that was dragging him down.

Based on his usual pace, he needed to cross in front of the hotel in under 15 seconds. Buddy looked like he was going to lose; he didn't lose faith in Blackie, though. Roger pointed at Blackie with his beer.

Roger cheered. "He's not gonna make it. Told ya, he couldn't beat no white man."

Buddy shook his head. "It ain't over yet."

Roger laughed, "Larson would wipe the floor with that savage. He's the fastest man alive."

Buddy pursed his lips as if he'd smelled something bad. "He ain't faster than Blackie," the farmer responded.

Buddy pointed out at Blackie, struggling in the summer heat. Blackie wiped his forehead with the back of his arm and kept running. "Look at that, man. Savages just ain't built right for being athletes. That's why there ain't no good Indian athletes at the 'lympics."

Buddy walked away from the window. He didn't need to see Blackie get to the Tavern to know what happened. He heard Roger whooping and hollering. He walked over to the bar, where the bartender was polishing the silverware with an oily rag. Buddy slammed the mug down on the bar.

The bartender shrugged. "Your boy lose?"

Buddy mocked up a fake frown. "Gambling is illegal in these here parts. Just what are you accusing me of?"

The bartender, a man who could claim some Native heritage but couldn't tell you what tribe, just smiled. His name was John Looking Glass because of his supposed resemblance to the old Nez Perce war band leader.

Looking Glass poured more of the pungent steam beer into the mug and slapped it down on the bar. As Buddy headed back to his table, Looking Glass reached up over the mirror behind the bar and pulled down a flintlock rifle.

The rifle was a style of rifle called a Kentucky Rifle even though they were developed in Pennsylvania. Looking Glass called it the Expedition Rifle because he'd been told that it had been involved in the Lewis and Clark Expedition around 1804. He'd doubted that, but the drunk who'd sold it to him needed the money, and Looking Glass thought it would look nice above his bar. The thing hadn't been shot in he didn't know how long, but he liked to keep it nice. With the same oily rag, he was using to clean the silverware, he wiped down the rifle. He buffed the curly maple stock until the wood gleamed so bright he could see the gaslights dancing in the shimmer. The rifle was inlaid with brass that had to be constantly polished. The oily smoke of the gaslights tarnished brass embarrassingly quickly. The brass was carved with an intricate relief map of the United States as Lewis and Clark imagined it. They were wrong about some of the finer details, but they got pretty close.

As he polished it, Looking Glass traced the bumpy metal map with his rag. He ran the oily rag down the barrel until it shimmered too. He put the flintlock back on the hooks above the bar.

Looking Glass shouted across the bar to Buddy, "You really think an Indian could beat a white man?"

II

President Thomas Jefferson couldn't calm down. He paced back and forth in the hallway, lurking in the glow of the candles. The carpet of the White House was new enough that his pacing was leaving footprints in the nap of the carpet. He carved the same path back and forth in the hallway, mumbling to himself, while gesturing with his hands. He was going over the same speech in his head, just letting it slip out of his mouth at a low volume. He mimed the gestures he would make while he was speaking. The whole time he was revising the speech and the gestures as he did so. Jefferson knew he was about to change the world; he just didn't know if it was about to be for the better or the worse. The United States had been a project he'd help give birth to.

George Washington had set the model for the statesman patriot; he served his country for eight years and retired quietly to Mount Vernon. In fact, he'd never wanted the job in the first place. The country had wanted and needed him. When he stepped aside after his second term, the old men of Europe were confused. He was loved by everyone, elected without contest, and given a mandate to govern. He could have stayed in office until his last breath, the way the royals of Old Europe might. But this was America. He'd stepped aside. Washington had built the country, they said.

If Washington had fathered America, John Adams was its first teacher. Revolutions don't die under the leadership of the first revolutionary. They died in the handing of the power. The people who had fought, died, sacrificed, and struggled for the first leader might feel abandoned when he handed power to someone else. Adams had held the country together though. He'd held it tightly and even built the White House. He'd only lived there for a year before leaving. Now, Jefferson was pacing the hallway, carving a path in the carpet. He still thought of the White House as Adams' house and the United States as Washington's country. But he was about to make the United States his own country. With a few scratches of a quill, he was going to double the size of the United States. It was going to be unrecognizable to anyone who had fought the revolution a few decades before.

France's own revolution was sputtering and floundering; they needed an injection of capital. Jefferson needed something that would unite the different states into one country. They still saw themselves as a bunch of different states with a few common interests; he needed to make them into one people with a few petty differences. The French had just regained control of Louisiana from the Spanish, but they were ready to leave the New World behind. This was going to be a monumental step into making the New World completely American. An empire was waiting, but the question remained: was it even France's to sell?

About 60,000 recognized people lived in Louisiana at the time. Half of them were descendants of Europeans, mostly French and Spanish, but the other 30,000 or so were African slaves. They'd been dragged from their homes and shoved in the bottom of boats. When they crawled out of the dysentery-laden hell, they were in a foreign country. What right did Jefferson have to tell them they were suddenly Americans? He worried about the slaves and the French taxpayers, but they weren't the ones that kept him awake at night. It was the Indians.

In 1776, he'd written about the "merciless Indian savages" in the Declaration of Independence. Almost thirty years later, they were still keeping him pacing the halls. The French -- and the Spanish before them -- had set up most of their settlements along the coast or along the banks of the Mississippi River. Depending on where the settlements were, the Indians typically kept strict rules about how far into the wilderness white people were allowed to travel. Once you got out of sight of a European settlement, you were just as likely to be in Indian Territory. In most parts of Louisiana, they greatly outnumbered the French or the Spanish. So, he was set to buy Louisiana from the French, when it didn't really even belong to them.

It belonged to the Chickasaw, the Choctaw, the Creeks, Sioux, and a hundred other tribes throughout the area. During the revolution, some of them had been friends. Some of them had sided with the French. In all honesty, the greatest gift many of them had given the fledgling republic was their neutrality. The Natives west of the Mississippi River had been begged, bribed, and threatened into neutrality in many cases. That allowed the South Carolinians and Georgians to focus on sending troops north to fight Great Britain. If the Chickasaws or the Creek Confederation had moved on the Southern Colonies, the colonists would have likely lost. Now, Jefferson was about to purchase their land from people who had no real claim to it. Was that an insult to the Natives who made the republic possible? Was he their liberator? Or was he just a new conqueror?

Those were only a few of the thoughts occupying his mind. He also wondered whether he had the power to purchase Louisiana. There really wasn't much in the Constitution about acquiring new land. He'd helped write the Constitution, but they hadn't been able to come to a conclusion at the convention. Worried that little things would derail the birth of the republic, they'd tabled a lot of discussions. Now, wrapped in the uncertain power of the United States presidency, he wondered if he could even make the deal he was about to make. If he did make it and the states decided he didn't have the authority after all, what would happen then? The United States, after all, was meant to be a collaboration of all of the states to share power with the federal government. If he bought this massive stretch of wilderness, it wouldn't be a state. It would be federal land. The federal government would own a stretch of land larger than the existing states, and it wouldn't have even asked them about that. What would that mean for states' power? They were begging for him to do something, though.

Begging was too gentle a word, Jefferson thought. They were demanding he do something. Shays' Rebellion and the Whiskey Rebellion were barely a decade old. The flames that had burned in those rebellions had dwindled to embers, but they were still flickering at the edges of the country. The French had moved back into Louisiana four years ago. It was mostly unremarked on in the Northeast, but in the South, it was causing chaos. Napoleon was stomping proudly over the New World and Europe. He'd outlawed slavery in different colonies and in France proper. The slaveholders in the Southern United States worried that he would outlaw slavery in New Orleans and the rest of Louisiana. That would deal a serious blow to the slave trade of the new states, but more importantly, to the mind of slaveholders at least, it would create dissent among their slaves. If slaves in Georgia knew they could gain freedom by fleeing to Louisiana, they would be much more likely to risk it. Even worse, they might start to demand abolition right in their home states.

To the minds of the slaveholders, a free Louisiana was a risk they couldn't afford. Jefferson was desperate to appease them. The Southerners were descendants of the Scots and the Irish; they'd bristled at British rule for four hundred years in their home countries, and they'd only grown more distrustful of powerful faraway governments. If he didn't calm them, they might cause problems. Even worse, they might rebel or secede. The ties that bound the South to the rest of the country were threadbare.

All of the handwringing and pacing was a wasted effort anyway. Jefferson had sent Livingston to purchase New Orleans for $10 million to keep the slaveholders from revolting. Also, it would have added another warm water port for the United States. Livingston had come back to inform Jefferson he had bought the entire Territory of Louisiana. The deal was already signed; that's how confident Livingston had been that he would accept the deal. Jefferson was backed into a corner. He couldn't allow America to back out of its commitment to the French, though. The republic was too new to be seen as feckless. He braced himself and started the walk towards the U.S. Capitol. The Senate would not be so easily moved.

─────

The Liksiyu was pulled from his sleep by strong forces. He felt himself hauled off his bed by invisible hands. He didn't know why but he thought the hands of ghosts would be cold; they weren't. Instead, they were warm and soft and reminded him of being a child in his mother's arms. Gently, the hands pressed on his back, forcing him out of his teepee into the bracing night air.

Night in the Pacific Northwest was damp and chilly, with the moist night air hanging like a cloud. He knew he should be cold, but instead, he felt completely comforted. He was wrapped in an unseen blanket and moved by unseen hands. He stumbled barefoot over the craggy rock at the edge of the water until he was on a cliff by the oceanside. He didn't know how long he'd been stumbling in front of the invisible hands, but there he was. Slippery moss oozed between his toes on the edge of the slimy rock. The ocean, some untold distance below him, was black. He could barely make it out, but he could hear the waves talking as if they were alive. The ocean inhaled as the water rolled out to sea and sighed as they splattered again against the rock. The hands seemed to press on his shoulders, so he sat. There he listened to the ocean, inhaling and moaning. To his ear, the ocean sounded sad. It seemed to say to him That they were on a precipice. His feet dangled over the edge of the cliff, lifeless in the night air, but that wasn't the edge. They were on the edge of something greater and more dangerous than any slip and fall from a rock.

The peace he felt in the hands of the unseen hands started to fade. Instead, he felt the pressing anxiety coming from the ocean. The inhale and exhale of the tide started speeding up until it was moving as quick as his pulse. Inhale. Sigh. Inhale. Sigh. It was growing quicker. His own breathing sped up until he couldn't get the breath out of his lungs fast enough. His throat shrank until breathing was a feat of strength. He felt himself growing distant. His head thumped with the frenzied pace of his heartbeat. He looked down and found himself standing over his own body.

There, on the edge of the cliff, the Liksiyu sat quietly staring sightless out into the ocean. But the other Liksiyu, looked down at himself. Behind him, he saw the unseen hands for the first time. They were not hands; they were men and women. Some he recognized and some he didn't. He recognized one of them -- a man in a white cotton shirt and buckskin leggings. He had a band of red paint painted across his eyes the way the desert Apache did.

Another one of the unseen hands was a woman. She was short and thin, with her ribs pressing against her skin underneath the furs she wore wrapped around herself. The Liksiyu couldn't recognize what kind of animal she could possibly be wearing, but he thought she must come from somewhere cold. She had to be one of the Indians who lived across the land on the other coast. The East coast was cold and windy. The wind whipping off the ocean was damp and chilly. These were the Natives who had been forced off their land first when the white people landed. She stared at the ground, not looking up to meet his eyes.

There were other Natives he didn't recognize -- a head-man wearing the loose clothes and light cotton of some of the Southern coastal tribes. They were still fighting a noble battle against the advance of white conquerors. This native, from one of the tribes the Liksiyu didn't recognize in the South, spoke first.

He held up his hands to show they were empty of weapons. "Do you know what has happened?" He asked the Liksiyu.

The Liksiyu meant to shake his head, but nothing happened. He wasn't a body anymore. His body was still sitting by the edge of the water, staring into the darkness.

The apparition of himself didn't move but somehow the man knew what he was saying.

The Native the Liksiyu didn't recognize spoke again. "They came, the white men did. They claimed they were coming with peace in mind; they showed me open hands but kept knives behind their backs. My people, the Catawba, were the most powerful tribe in our area. We made a fatal mistake; we trusted them. They were not peaceful -- they were outnumbered." The Catawba opened his shirt to show a bloody, gaping wound in his chest. The wound wept blood down his shirt. It never stopped bleeding.

The Catawba kept talking. "They brought smallpox. Some of their own died from the disease, but the Catawba suffered more greatly. When we were brought low by illness, they came with guns. They pushed us from our land and claimed we were the ones making war. We made deals with them. When they wanted to expand, they did. They had no respect for the Catawba or their own deals. By the time we realized they would never be satisfied, we were almost all dead. Do you know what has happened?"

Somewhere in the back of his mind, the Liksiyu recognized that he was speaking a language that wasn't his own. The Catawba was speaking the language of his people, but the Liksiyu understood it perfectly.

The woman in the furs spoke next. "I am a Monacan. We lived in the Country of the People of the Land. Two hundred years ago, we discovered the white people who would come to conquer our country. They made peace at first, but they quickly drove us from our land until it was filled only with white faces. This is what they seek -- a land of only white faces. When the colonists split with their home country, we fought with the British. The British promised to take no more of our land. We didn't believe them, but we feared the colonists more. When the

British lost, we lost. Most of our country fled north to the remaining British colonies. The rest were absorbed. Do you know what has happened?"

The Liksiyu spoke back to the Monacan woman in her native language. He'd never spoken it before, but it flowed off his tongue. "Is that what will happen to me? Will we be absorbed?"

The Monacan woman never looked up from the ground. "If you are lucky."

"If we are unlucky?" The Liksiyu asked.

A Native the Liksiyu didn't recognize whispered, "Annihilation."

The Liksiyu sighed. "Who will bring this annihilation?"

The Catawba hissed, "The American headman, Thomas Jefferson."

The Liksiyu asked, "Why would he do this when we have done nothing to him?"

The Catawba replied, "He wants a country of only white faces. You have no place in his country."

"This is my country. He has no place in it."

The Natives all laughed at once. Their laughter sounded like dry leaves rustling in a stiff wind. They quickly fell silent. The Catawba said, "It is their country now. The ones with guns make laws."

"We will get guns."

"Not enough," The Catawba replied.

Then the Liksiyu was back to sitting next to the ocean in his body. He looked around. The spirits of the other Natives had disappeared, and he couldn't hear the ocean anymore. There was only a fire crackling next to him. Where had the fire come from? The Liksiyu stood up and walked over to the fire.

He felt no heat coming from it. The red-orange flames danced and frolicked, spitting the occasional sparks into the air, but it gave off no heat and no light. Looking into the flames, the light burned his eyes, but as soon as he looked outside of it, there was only blackness. He felt like that fire -- a flame dancing in the darkness. He inhaled and sighed the way the ocean had. What had happened?

He put his hand in the fire and felt nothing. He held his hand there. When he pulled it out, his hand was unburnt. Fire without heat and flames without light. He was that fire. He sat down next to the fire.

He asked the fire, "Do you know what has happened?"

The wood popped and spit out a jet of sparks as a response. He didn't know if it was yes or no, but he thought the fire knew.

He spoke into the fire again. "Something has happened. All that I knew will soon end."

The bill had been passed back and forth between the House and Senate more times than Jefferson cared to count. Sometimes, Thomas Jefferson hated the republic he had helped create. There was never a doubt in his mind that the republican system of government was the only one that could make a population truly free, but sometimes, he definitely envied the conquerors, despots, and kings. He even was a little bit jealous of King George III. He'd been king for decades by the time the American colonists decided to rebel. He'd been the king who lost half of the British Crown colonies, but he was king. In fact, he was King of Great Britain when the colonials had rebelled. Now, he was King of the United Kingdom of Great Britain and Ireland. He had lost lucrative colonies all over the world and somehow managed to not only keep his job, but to expand his power.

Standing out in the hallway of the Senate chamber,

Jefferson couldn't help but chuckle a little bit to himself. He imagined what would have happened to him if he had lost half of the United States. *What would become of the president who presided over a split in the United States?* He thought. He assumed the president who lost half of the states would be reviled as the worst president in history. He would never have been re-elected. He might even have been impeached and removed. Not a king, though. A king could just decree a thing and everyone had to fall in line. *Look at me now,* he thought. He was standing out in the hallway of the Senate chamber because the US president had to ask permission to even be allowed on the floor of Congress. *I can't imagine King George ever has to wait in the hallway of Parliament,* he thought and chuckled to himself a little bit. He was a servant of the people, he told himself, but many days, he felt like a servant to the thirty-four senators sitting in that chamber.

Pacing in the hallway felt like the sum total of everything he did as President. He often joked in private that he should have given himself more power when they were writing the constitution. Just then the door to the Senate chamber opened and a young aide stepped out into the hallway. Jefferson stopped his pacing and waited for the boy.

The boy cleared his throat. "Uh, Mr. President…"

"Yes?"

The boy said, "The bill passed. You bought Louisiana, sir."

In the far Northwest on the edge of the Pacific Ocean, a rain had started to fall. The Liksiyu wasn't cold, despite the icy rain. Then, as if it had never existed, the fire vanished. He knew nothing about the men in the United

States Senate and the House of Representatives. He didn't know they'd made a decision to buy a massive stretch of land they didn't even own. But somehow, that fact traveled on the wind and extinguished his fire. Even if someone had explained to the Liksiyu what had happened, it's not clear he would have even understood. In the Louisiana Territory -- as the white people called it -- there were dozens of different tribes of Natives. Every tribe controlled a stretch of territory that was their country. The borders of countries shifted and morphed and were often disputed, but they were very real.

Despite all of that, despite the hundreds of different shifting borders, the French had drawn an imaginary line on a piece of paper in France and called it La Louisiane. Those borders weren't real borders -- they weren't rivers, fences, bridges, or anything you could touch. They were just ink. Ink on paper. Would the Liksiyu understand that the United States had just conquered hundreds of countries without mustering a single war party? The men in suits in the United States Senate didn't understand it. Why should the Liksiyu?

III

Meriwether Lewis and William Clark were highly respected and very well recommended. Jefferson had been told, in no uncertain terms, that these men could explore the great, untamed wilderness that he had just purchased. Jefferson had known Meriwether for a few years at that point. Lewis had been an aide in the White House for a while, even living there along with the President.

Meriwether Lewis, a Virginian by birth, shared an instant kinship with President Jefferson from the first time they'd met -- Virginia had a way of attracting that kind of devotion. Meriwether Lewis wasn't only a Virginian, though. He'd cut his teeth in the Georgia backcountry as a boy. He learned trapping, hunting, foraging, and fishing. If his heart was Virginian, then his hands and feet were Georgian. That kind of knowledge would help him hack his way through the Louisiana wilderness. Georgia wasn't Louisiana, but they both shared the same kind of rugged humidity and muggy swamp feel.

Meriwether Lewis stepped into the Oval Office. He had a tall, thin man in tow. Lewis jabbed a thumb in the direction of the tall man.

"This is William Clark," Lewis said.

Clark bowed his head as if he were bowing after a

theater performance. Jefferson chuckled. He extended a hand and said, "We usually just settle for shaking hands." Clark cleared his throat. "Oh, um, yes sir, Mr. President. We don't get a lot of presidents in Kentucky." Jefferson shrugged. "I like Kentucky. I'll try to visit before I leave office."

"That'd be great, Mr. President."

The Corps of Discovery, as Lewis and Clark's group was officially called, was about to set off with a simple task that was actually quite complex. In a vague sense, they were supposed to travel throughout the Louisiana Purchase and see what the hell Jefferson had actually bought. The people who had bought Louisiana, the American people, had a right to know what their tax dollars had paid for. He'd leveraged the full faith and credit of the United States on a stretch of unexplored land. They deserved to know what plants and animals lived there. More than that, they deserved to know how their president planned to get their money back.

With the density of the wilderness and the wide stretch of different climates throughout the territory, Meriwether assured Jefferson that there was going to be plenty of economic opportunity for the United States. Jefferson hoped so or he'd be leaving Washington, D.C. under cover of darkness.

President Jefferson's face turned serious, the way it always did when he had to discuss matters of statecraft. "Lewis," he said, "I managed to shake those hard hearts in Congress for $2,500."

Lewis sucked his teeth with his tongue the way he did when he was thinking. He pulled Clark aside. They talked quietly to each other. Whatever they were talking about, Lewis was talking while Clark did the math in his head. He counted off something on his fingertips. They whispered a little more, then they nodded in agreement.

Lewis came back and said, "Mr. President, we need another $22."

Jefferson scoffed and shook his head. "Can't happen. You don't know what I went through to get this from Congress."

"Sir, it's only $22," Lewis said.

Jefferson gritted his teeth. He was obviously starting to get angry in a hurry. Through his clenched teeth, he hissed, "Congress won't move on this. Not possible."

"Sir..." Lewis started.

That's when the dam broke. Ever since he was a child, Thomas Jefferson had struggled with a speech impediment; he was a stammerer. He tried his best for his entire life to beat his stuttering problem, and he'd been pretty successful. He avoided certain words or phonemes that he knew would be a stumbling block for him. He'd been doing it for so long that he didn't even think about it; it had become automatic. There was one weakness in his armor, though. When he became angry, he would lose it. He'd forget to avoid certain words, he'd forget to speak slow enough to sound out every word, and he'd start stuttering the way he had when he was a child.

This boy, not even thirty years old yet, had done it.

"Meriwether," Jefferson shouted much louder than he intended. "You have no idea what I've been through with this damned Congress. I sent a man to purchase one port city. One port. What did he come back with? An entire god-forsaken territory filled with Lord knows how many savages. I can barely govern the states we have now and I'm expected to govern some stretch of Abaddon neither the French nor the Spanish could manage to control."

With his normal calm demeanor broken, he started

stuttering. "When the c..c..colonists decided to fight against the most puh..puh...powerful King in the world, they looked to Thomas Jefferson to declare our independence. Now, they wah...wah...want me to again do the impossible. To govern the ungovernable. Wh..wh..wh..why, in the name of all the angels in heaven, do you need $22? Your answer beh..beh..better be unfathomably convincing or so help me..."

By now, his lips and chin were slathered with his own saliva from screaming. His face was red and his eyes were bulging in his head. His hair had been thrown askew and sweat was starting to build on his forehead.

Meriwether had never seen the President lose his temper like that. It was unsettling. He sank his head and lowered his shoulders and took the abuse. With his head still ducked, afraid to make eye contact with the fuming president, Meriwether put two fingers in his mouth, pulled his lips tight, and pealed out a loud droning whistle. The president's eyes narrowed. He looked ready to lunge out with a fist. In the tense silence, they all heard it. Pat... pat... pat... The sound of pattering feet grew closer and closer. It was a sound of feet slapping the carpet outside the oval office. When the footfalls seemed impossibly close, a slobbering Newfoundland dog came bounding through the open door. It's hair, black as night and shaggy like unkempt grass, flopped like curtains in a stiff breeze. The dog, as tall on its hind legs as President Jefferson and probably just as heavy, galumphed into the room. It reared up on his hind legs, slapping its front paws on the President's shoulder. He took a step back, staggering under the weight of the dog. Meriwether gasped. The dog dragged its massive tongue over the President's face, smearing his beard to his face. The slobbering grew intense enough that drool ran down Jefferson's face. The dog didn't stop though; he slathered the President of the United States in his slobber.

The president opened his mouth as if he were about to scream, but instead, a loud breathless laughter escaped. He inhaled and guffawed. He ran his hands through the shaggy coat of the dark dog, ruffling the hair in unkempt tufts. He laughed and laughed and laughed. When finally the dog fell back to all fours, Jefferson rooted around in the pocket of his pants. He pulled out a wadded handful of greenbacks.

He counted out twenty-two dollars, laughing the whole time. He flicked the money in Meriwether's direction. "Take it. Oh Lord above, just take it." President Jefferson clapped Meriwether on the shoulder. "Let me see this team you've assembled."

A few days later, Meriwether Lewis and William Clark returned to the Oval Office with their full retinue of core explorers. There were thirty-three of them in all. Well, thirty-three white men and six slaves. So, thirty-nine if you were counting the slaves, but rarely did they count the slaves. They put them in the same side of the ledger as the horses or the cowhide coats. They were commodities. That was actually one of the things that had led President Jefferson to purchase Louisiana -- the Catholics. The damn Papists. They had taken to baptizing the slaves while the French and Spanish Catholics controlled Louisiana. They baptized Negro and Native slaves alike. The slaveholders in the American South were shaken up by this because it meant one thing: if the Catholics baptized their slaves, it meant they thought the slaves could be saved and go to heaven. If they could be saved by Christ's grace, they must have souls. If they have souls, they're no different than white men and they shouldn't be enslaved. The very idea of baptizing the slaves was dangerous to the institution of slavery throughout the United States. Lewis and Clark would quickly find that the Louisiana territory was foreign in more ways than they were quite prepared to understand.

Matthias Dimke would not be surprised by La Louisiane, though. He'd spent his years in the US Cavalry making a name for himself as an expert horseman and an expert in Indian affairs. He was a loyal US cavalryman but he was French Canadian. That made him an exact contrast of the Southerners Lewis and Clark. They'd grown up on the southern and eastern edge of French and Spanish Louisiana. Dimke had grown up on the northern and western edge of Louisiana. He was fluent in the garbled French the Canadians and Louisianans spoke. In fact, Lewis made a habit of joking about Dimke's accent. It sounded like he had mouth full of hardtack and a stuffed nose. He was an invaluable resource, though. He'd spent his time in the U.S. War Department dealing with Indian affairs.

As their horses assembled in the fort at St. Charles, their hooves sank into the mud under the weight of man and horseflesh. Meriwether Lewis and William Clark sat astride their two painted mares. The horses were siblings, if they could be called that. Mares of the same brood. They were almost identical, fifteen hands high each. Lewis and Clark each wore the stripes and insignias on their Army uniforms signifying their rank. Clark kept a Kentucky rifle stuffed in a long holster at the front of the horse's saddle. The rifle, brand new, was polished with a gleam on the cherry wood that caught the light and shimmered.

As the Missouri sunlight bounced off the polished brass, it hit Lewis in the eye.

He chuckled to Clark. "That thing is so clean, I reckon you've never shot it."

Clark ticked an eyebrow up. "I sure have. In Kentucky, we learn to take care of what little we have."

Lewis nodded. "Maybe, when we get to the edge of the Louisiana territory, I'll have that thing engraved with something to commemorate the journey."

Clark replied, "That won't be necessary, sir. I can't imagine anyone will care about a few fool Southerners who went out into the wilderness."

Dimke, overhearing them, walked his horse up next to them. "Au contraire. I suspect, we might never die. Not in people's memories at least."

Lewis chuckled to himself and gigged his horse. "We're like to die in about three days' time."

Three days wasn't an arbitrary number of days in Lewis' mind. They were in St. Charles, Missouri, gathering in a muddy field under the summer sun. The mud at the frontier fort stank of horse dung and human sweat. It was the last outpost they had, though. Three days' ride west they would encounter the very last European or American settlement in the United States. That still felt weird to think. He was ankle deep in uncultivated muck, but this was the United States. He would soon find that it was only the United States in the minds of Americans and mapmakers. To the Natives, it was still Chickasaw, Conecuh, Navajo, Creek, and a hundred others. And they were none too pleased to hear that they were supposedly American subjects. Looking back, some would say this was the beginning of the first genocide in world history. To Meriwether Lewis, William Clark, and the other fine young men from Kentucky, it was the beginning of a great adventure. The truth would probably get muddied some-where in the middle, but the Natives wouldn't get their side of it out truly. The genocides, assimilated, and con-quered don't write history, and no historian paints his side as the evil empire.

Meriwether Lewis was scared of the Natives in the wil-derness. As with everything living in the woods, they're more scared of you than you are of them.

Two of the other fine young men were from the War Department as well -- Sergeant David Dalton and Lieutenant Robert Allan. Allan spoke the language of the French Canadians, and Dalton often bragged he could sneak up on a deer while wearing a belt made of bells.

William Clark gigged his horse and rode it up to a slave who was carrying a heavy pack on his back, hunched against the weight of the pack. He wasn't wearing a hat like the white men were. The sun was beating against his forehead. William Clark rode up, looking down on the slave man. He pulled his rifle out of the saddle holster and held it down to the slave.

"Load this for me. 90 grains of black powder. 177 grain lead ball."

The slave took the rifle from him. The man looked down the rifle's barrel then glared up at Clark. He stood there for a moment -- both of them -- neither of them say-ing a word. They just stared at them. The white Army man on the horse and the black slave holding the rifle.

The slave broke the silence. "This sure is a nice rifle, sure. I imagine you could put a hole clean through a man. Be dead before he hit the ground, I 'spect."

When Grey Snow had been young, there were hundreds of Niutachi Indians. They were everyone he knew, and his world never stretched much farther than the river mouth. That's who they were, the Niutachi. They were people who lived at the mouth of the river. The river, the one the white men called the Missouri River, was the lifeblood of his entire tribe. It was the artery that pumped life to every corner of their part of the world, and he never strayed very far from it. There wasn't much reason to. Now, in his early twenties, there were only a few hundred Niutachi -- probably about 300. He knew every single one of them by sight. He never met anyone he hadn't met before. Not Niutachi at least. The only strangers he met came in the night.

They came in the night, whooping and hollering. Their arrowheads and knives flashing silver in the gray moonlight. They were usually the Sauk and the Fox tribesmen. The fighting men of the Sauk and the Fox were to be respected; they were some of the most fearsome he'd ever encountered. That's not to say the Niutachi were always beaten by the Sauk and the Fox. Many times, Grey Snow found himself on the winning side of skirmishes. More often than not, they would leave before much blood had been shed. Their horses stolen or cut loose, and their children kidnapped. That's why Grey Snow was on the Eastern side of the River the White men called the Missouri. He normally hunted on the western side of the River. Today, though, he didn't want to encounter the Sauk and the Fox. His tribe had begged for peace with the Sauk recently by ceding the hunting grounds on the western side of the river mouth. It was an embarrassment but there weren't enough Niutachi to mount an effective defense. So they hung their heads.

Grey Snow was lucky. A heavy rain a few days ago

had sent the river swelling and spilling water all over the plains. The grass that bloomed a few days later brought the buffalo who would normally only be on the western side to the Eastern side. He could finally hunt them and possibly feed his entire tribe for a few days. He was going to be a hero. He sat on the back of his panting horse with its scrawny breasts and protruding ribs. The horse chewed grass as if it hadn't eaten in months. It might not have. He couldn't remember the last time the grass had been blooming on that side of the river. So he couldn't be sure of the last time the horse actually got to eat. Judging by its scrawny legs, it had been a while. These were the lean times for everyone though. Grey Snow could feel his heart beating in his stomach, yearning for something to fill it. He hadn't eaten in a day and a half. His musket, stolen off the bleeding corpse of a Frenchman about 80 years ago, was well-kept and well-oiled but there was only enough shot and gunpowder for one shot. He'd melted his little brothers toy soldier down into a scattering of pellets he hoped was heavy enough to take down a buffalo.

Sitting on the back of his eating horse, he felt himself instinctively synchronizing his breathing with that of his horse. The buffalo, a group of about six of them, trundled across the open plain. They were fat and happy, probably moving from a side of the river still flourishing with grass. A part the drought hadn't touched the way it had Grey Snow's piece of the river. There, at the back of the pack, was one that limped as it walked. One of its hind legs was injured, and it looked a little bit larger than the rest. To Grey Snow's mind that was the sign of an old buffalo -- one that would be easy to kill.

He took a deep breath, adjusted the blanket serving as a saddle. He got himself setting properly. If he didn't do this properly, when he broke into a gallop, he'd bruise every muscle in his hips and thighs. He took another deep breath, grabbed the attention of his horse with a jerk of the reins and kicked it into action. The horse hesitant at first, sprang into a canter. He kicked it again and it galloped forward. He let out a war whoop and settled the musket under his shoulder. The horse sprinted forward. Grey Snow kept his head low and his hips centered. The wind whipped through his long braid, yanking his hair in every direction.

He let out another war whoop to scatter the buffalo. The pack of buffalo took off sprinting. Every time he saw he it, he was surprised. The buffalo were a lot faster than their hefty body would have suggested. All except the old one at the back of the pack that was. That one tried his hardest to rumble away from the whooping Niutachi, but couldn't get away. It hobbled more than anything. As Grey Snow approached the pack, he settled his feet into the stirrups and got his balance. He stood up in stirrups. He dropped the reins but the horse knew what to do. It curved around and took a line parallel to the hobbling buffalo. Grey Snow put the musket to his shoulder and tried to sight down the lines. He bent his knees to counteract the frantic rocking of the horse. Finally, with a breath held then slowly releasing, he got the buffalo in his sights. He slowly let his breath out and squeezed the trigger.

Before he could get the trigger depressed, he heard that telltale thunder. The buffalo twitched and moaned. It whined and bucked, kicking its hind legs into the air. It tried to storm off but only got a few steps before it slowed, rocked from side to side, then collapsed onto its side.

Grey Snow's mouth fell open. The chest of the buffalo sagged as its last breath escaped. Grey Snow just stared down at the dead buffalo. He looked at the flintlock of his musket to make sure he hadn't somehow fired his load.

He hadn't. The flintlock was still cocked back. He looked around. Then he saw it.

A white man rode up on a horse. The man was wearing a dingy woven shirt, stained with sweat under the arms and down the front. He was wearing heavy canvas pants the color of dirt. He had a gleaming rifle, the kind they made in Kentucky. It was shimmering with brass embellishments polished to a high shine.

The man rode up out of the woods and put the rifle back in the holster on his saddle.

He rode up to the buffalo and his horse stood over it. The man leaned over his saddle, crossing his arms. Grey Snow felt his finger twitching against the trigger. He could kill this white man and take his kill. Grey Snow knew something though; white men were never alone. Somewhere not far was a whole posse of them. Maybe even the US Army.

The man held up a hand. "Bonjour."

A Frenchman, Grey Snow thought. His hair was the color of steel and gold; Grey Snow had never seen a golden-haired Frenchman before but anything was possible with these white people. Grey Snow spoke almost exclusively Chiwere, the language of his people, but he knew a little bit of French. Enough for trading.

He put the musket across his lap and held up his empty hands. "Bonjour, mon nom est La Neige Grise."

"Ravi de vous rencontrar. Mon nom est Meriwether Lewis. Bienvenue aux Etats-Unis."

Not a Frenchman at all. An American.

IV

Blackie Sullivan ran through town with a purse slung over his shoulder to his opposite hip. The heavy purse banged against his hip with every stride. He wore his shirt unbuttoned down to the bottom of his sternum, his chest slippery with sweat, and his hair pulled back in a messy braid. His feet slapped the dusty road in his sandals. He was pretty sure he could have rung out his braided hair like a waterlogged shirt. The temperature had been climbing all summer and they were worried it would never break. The locals called it "Indian Summer." Blackie didn't really understand what that could possibly mean. Indians didn't like the oppressive heat any more than he did. In fact, he'd learned the term "oppressive heat" from his father. His father, the last full-blooded Cayuse Indian, had died two years ago, and Blackie still felt a pang of pain when he thought of him. He could still imagine his dad was sitting in the cool air of a tavern sipping iced tea.

His father defined oppressive heat as that temperature it gets when you don't want to do anything; when you don't want to go to the store or even get out of bed. He joked that it was oppressive because the white men wouldn't let them move around in town -- just like the heat. Blackie lived outside of town for just that reason. He was in town today to buy groceries, though. He had a cabin up in the mountains that covered just about everything he needed, but there were some things he couldn't' grow up there. He had rows of vegetables that had just started to ripen in the sun. He had money, though, and was in the mood for beef.

Earlier that day, he'd delivered a block of ice to Mister John's Butchery. The keeper of the butcher shop, Mr. John, had been just hooking a side of beef in the freezer when Blackie had run up. The side of beef, easily two hundred pounds had proven too unwieldy for the aging Mr. John. Blackie had put his shoulder to the side of cow and helped the man get it up on the hook and wheel it into his icebox. In exchange, Mr. John said he'd give Blackie a real good deal on some beef.

Blackie slowed down to a walk as he got to the door of Mister John's. He pushed open the doors, and the bell above the door jingled as he walked in. Mister John was standing behind the counter, smoking a skinny cigarette rolled from some butcher paper. Mister John smiled. His teeth were stained with a sooty nicotine sunrise.

"Blackie, by God, how the hell are ya."

Blackie waved to Mr. John. "I'm doing pretty good. How's the beef today?"

Mister John laughed. "That cow must have been treated like the Queen of Sheba. It's so tender, I threw away my knife. Just gonna use a spoon from here on out." It was the same thing Mr. John said about every shipment of meat he got.

Truth was, the meat that made it all the way up to Walla Walla was usually tough as shoe leather. There were always a couple of good cuts on the cow but that sort of thing went to his regular customers or to the territorial governor. The ones he sold to the few Indians who came in were usually shoulder cuts. They were hefty hunks of meat that could be used as door stoppers more than anything else. The flavor was good though. The shoulder meat had the most blood vessels and proteins, making it the most flavorful.

Mister John put down his cigarette and held up his knife. "Hold on right there. I'm gonna cut you a prime piece."

Blackie laughed at the knife. "Thought you were putting your knives away."

Mr. John shrugged. "Oh this is just for picking my teeth."

He made a show of picking at his teeth with the hefty meat cleaver. He disappeared into the ice box. Blackie set his purse up on the counter, sweeping away a sprinkling of cigarette ash to find a clean spot.

Mr. John came back from the ice box with a bleeding chunk of meat. He slapped the meat down on the counter. Mr. John pulled back his cleaver and brought it down like a hammer. The cleaver slapped against the counter and the meat fell away into two equal parts. Mr. John yanked a piece of butcher paper and wrapped up one of the hunks with the practiced excellence of a skilled professional. With a piece of twine, he wrapped it up and slid it across the counter to Blackie. The entire butchering and packing process probably took Mr. John about twenty seconds. It was nothing if not impressive.

"How much do I owe you?" Blackie asked.

Mr. John picked up the piece of meat and placed it on a scale next to his box of rolled cigarettes. The scale depressed like a plunger when the meat slapped down onto the cold metal. The needle on the scale swung up to about three pounds. It bounced around before settling right under three pounds. This was the veiny, muscly meat of the shoulder. Mr. John charged nineteen cents per pound for this type of meat. He probably should charge less, but shipping meat all the way out to the hinterlands of Walla Walla wasn't the easiest thing in the world, and the prices went up. If you were buying this same cut of meat in California, it would probably cost about sixteen cents a pound. This wasn't California, though. This was the frontier. So, it was nineteen cents a pound, plus the cost of getting your teeth fixed at the dentist after tugging on that stringy hunk of cow. But that was the white person's price. That wasn't the price he charged savages.

He looked down his nose at Blackie Sullivan. The man's coal black hair was pulled into a messy braid that ran down his back all the way to his butt. It was sweaty and stringy, like he'd dipped himself in the Walla Walla River. The sweat trickled down his forehead, tracing a course around his nose. He wiped it whenever it got too close to his nose. His shirt was stained with sweat to the point that it clung to his chest and armpits. This wasn't the first time either. Mr. John could tell that he was accustomed to this kind of sweating by the lines of salt all over the shirt, like sand at the coast of the beach. Old sweat had dried ages ago, but left behind the salt in the form of stained white lines. Mr. John tried to gauge how much people would be able to pay so he could charge them a little extra and take home a little more off the top. He looked at Blackie Sullivan and thought the man had to be dirt poor. Chances are, he didn't have a pot to piss in or a window to throw it out of. Mr. John took a little bit of pity on the man.

He wrinkled his nose. "That'll be 59 cents, son." He charged him the nineteen cents a pound he charged white men. Mr. John thought to himself that he hoped Blackie didn't go blabbing about it, though. White men would never pay him nineteen cents again. They'd demand to be paid better than the savages living out in the wilderness. They weren't worth a damn bit more, but a white man loved nothing better than feeling superior to somebody. In the South, they looked down their noses at Negroes and women. That made them feel real good about themselves. Out here in the wind-spun, sand-swept Northwest, white men looked down at the natives. Oh, they liked that just fine. You were never so poor that you were at the bottom rung of the ladder. Mr. John had sold meat to a man the other day who didn't have two shoes. That's not a man who didn't have two pairs of shoes -- he didn't have one complete pair. He wore one shoe on his left foot and just kept his right foot wrapped up in rags.

He worked on a river barge on the near-by Columbia River and didn't wear shoes on the deck, so he couldn't really afford to pay for a pair of shoes that he'd only wear when he was on land. So, he didn't have a complete pair of shoes. That man still felt superior to the richest native in the world. And in the eyes of the law, he was. He was a lot better.

Blackie fished around in his money purse that hung at his hip. He came out with a palm-full of the most brilliant, shimmering yellow gold Mr. John had ever seen. The nugget of gold was about the size of Mr. John's thumb. It was dirty and covered in whatever kind of rock had surrounded it, but the gold still peaked out. It had the smooth, rounded edges of a rock that had been milled by a river. By the smoothness of the edges, Mr. John thought it had to be pretty close to the surface for the water to really smooth it this much. That meant this savage just had massive chunks of gold sitting on the edge of his stream for the taking. His stream, Mr. John thought and laughed. *About to be my damn stream.*

Mr. John held out his hand. Blackie dumped the nugget into the man's hand.

Blackie said, "This is all I have. How much is enough?"

Mr. John tried to hide his reaction. He tried to keep his eyes from widening or from openly salivating. He bounced the rock in his hand. It was heavier than he thought it was going to be. It was caught up in the ore from the river, but he thought there had to be at least two ounces of pure gold in there. Maybe one, if he was being conservative. He did the math in his head as quickly as he could. The U.S. government had set the price of gold at $20.67 per troy ounce a long time ago. He did his calculations. A troy ounce is about ten percent heavier than a normal ounce, so he would say this was probably closer to two troy ounces than one. At $20.67 per troy ounce, this rock was probably worth about $41. That was more than the butcher made in a normal month. Oh, he could work with this. He straightened his face and put a frown on.

"Well," Mr. John groaned, "I don't normally do this. I don't like it. But, you know what, Blackie? I like ya. I like ya a lot. I'll do ya this favor."

Blackie smiled. "Oh, thank you Mr. John. I appreciate it."

Mr. John frowned. "Mmmhmmm. You just get this converted to some greenbacks soon, ya hear?"

"Yessir."

Mr. John plopped the pebble onto the meat scale. The needle ticked over to 4 ounces. That was just a little under four troy ounces. He had to consider about half of the stone being ore and not gold. Yeah, he was looking at about $40 worth of gold.

Mr. John pulled out a meat tenderizing mallet from underneath the table. It was a heavy metal hammer with a flat face and gnarled teeth. Mr. John set the gold nugget on the table and studied it like a golfer setting a ball on the tee. With a grunt, he swung the metal mallet down on the nugget. The hammer rang out against the metal table with a clanking thud. The mallet jumped off the table. When he moved his hammer, the gold nugget had been split about perfectly in half. There was a fine dusting of gray rock and yellow gold, but it was mostly two halves. Mr. John had separated the rock into two equal parts -- a precision with his tools that he could have only learned from years as a butcher. He could take a meat cleaver and hack off a specific amount of meat with his eyes closed. You want two pounds of flank steak? He could slice you off two pounds with a precision that usually meant he got within about an ounce of his target. Depended on how aged the beef was.

He picked up the piece of gold and set it back on the scale. It was just under two ounces. Yeah, he did it perfectly.

He slid half of the gold into his pocket and pushed the other half back across the table to Blackie.

"There you go," he lied," That's about fifty-five cents worth of gold. I'll give you a little discount because we're such good buddies." It was a gross lie. He had about twenty dollars in gold in his pocket, but obviously, Blackie didn't know about gold. The only reason Mr. John knew the price of gold by memory was this uncle had been a jeweler and the price of gold hadn't changed since before the War Between the States. And most people couldn't eyeball the weight of something as easily as a butcher could. Most people didn't know what an ounce felt like by touch. You could hand a random person an ounce of gold and tell him it was eight ounces and they wouldn't know the different. The opposite was also true. Blackie probably had no idea he had two full ounces of pure gold in his hand, because he didn't know by feel what one ounce felt like.

Blackie smiled. He put the rest of his gold back in his pocket. He grabbed his paper wrapped meat and waved at Mr. John. "Thank you so much, Mr. John. You're a good guy."

Blackie waved again and ran out the door. The bell on the door jangled as he left. Mr. John thought the sound of the jangling bell sounded a lot like a cash register.

"Damn," he whispered to himself. He pulled the gold out of his pocket again and studied it. He whistled at the sheer luck of it all. $20 worth of gold. Damn. That's when he really started thinking. The gold was just sitting in that stream. Why should that injun have any more right to it than him? Indians thought they were living in harmony with the land, but what they were really doing was wasting it. If the land was going to give you buffaloes, then why should you act like eating that buffalo isn't part of being in harmony? Same was true with the gold. Blackie didn't know what to do with gold. That much was obvious. He just let himself get taken for $20 worth of gold and thanked Mr. John the whole time. He was probably pulling just enough out of the river to pay for meat and things.

Mr. John shook his head and muttered, "Indians don't know a damn thing about being good business folk. Gonna have to commandeer his little stream."

But where did Blackie live? No one had ever been to his home, obviously. Who would go to the home of an Indian? He just kind of appeared at the edge of town each morning, sprinting for the ice truck. He was always running; that's what made an impression on Mr. John. Every time he saw Blackie, he was running. He ran into town, ran around all day delivering ice, and then ran back into the woods. He was like a red-skinned ghost.

"Someone will have to track him to his teepee or what-ever the hell he got," muttered Mr. John to himself.

It couldn't be him though. Mr. John was about as round as he was tall and he loved his hand rolled cigarettes a little too much. He spent most of the day hacking and about half the time, he hacked up a stringy yellow goop. No, he wasn't much of a runner. He would have to recruit some folks to help him track down the Indian. He would need some quick footed fellows with hard hearts. Men who wanted to be rich. Out here in the steam beer world. In the hard scrabble, sand whipped Northwest, there was no shortage of men who were willing to chase a buck. These were the last frontiersmen and they wouldn't hesitate to take from an Indian. Shouldn't be hard at all.

Mr. John grabbed a smoke from his box of rolled ciga-rettes. He struck a match with his thumbnail, waited for the pungent sulfur to burn off, and touched it to the tip of his cigarette. He puffed until it came to life. Mr. John waddled his girth out the front door and latched it closed behind. He reckoned he could close up shop early now that he had $20 worth of gold in his pocket. Yeah, there wasn't much that could happen this day to top that. He waddled toward a pub, the Steamed Clam.

―――――――――――――

The Steamed Clam had been around for a few years; Mr. John remembered when it had been built. That was some-time around 1875. Mr. John chuckled. It seemed like the bar had just opened, but that was thirty-one years ago.

"Damn," he said to himself. "I'm getting old."

He was counting time in decades, not years anymore. However, his age never seemed more obvious than when he was trying to waddle his girth across the street. If he were still the young man who played rugby with his friends, he could chase Blackie back to his house all on his own and not have to split the money with some money-grubbers from the Steamed Clam. He wouldn't ever consider going to the other one, though.

He didn't dare go to the Look-See, though. That was the other bar on the other end of the street. People who had been there said the owner was a half-Indian himself. He even let Indians drink there. Just thinking about Indians mingling with white folks caused Mr. John to sweat and fume. He could feel the blood rising to his face as he clenched his teeth. Of course a half-Indian was fine with co-mingling of the races -- he was the result of that kind of mingling.

You didn't see rabbits with deer or squirrels with beards. "'Tain't natural," Mr. John muttered to himself as he walked into the bar.

A man sitting at a table by the bar looked up from his shimmering amber whiskey. The man, a young guy with a mop of floppy blond hair and the bulky shoulders of a railroad laborer, frowned. "What ain't?"

Mr. John spun around to see who'd spoken to him. "Say what, son?"

The man brushed his hair out of his eyes. "You said 'tain't natural'. What ain't?"

Mr. John grumbled, "Injuns with whites. Drinking, dancing, doing God only knows what."

The man turned the corner of his lip up towards his nose as if he smelled something foul. In the dank summer heat of the Steamed Clam, that was very likely. But he wasn't disgusted by any smell.

The man spat, "I tell you what, it 'bout sends me into a spitting rage every time I see a redskin with a white. Our fine white women being seduced by savages. With their long hair and their Injun charm. Makes me sick."

Mr. John smiled. *This is a man I can work with,* he thought.

Mr. John pulled out a chair at the table with the floppy-haired man. "You mind?" He asked.

The man shook his head and motioned for Mr. John to sit. The hefty man lowered himself into the chair. The wood seemed to groan under his bulk.

Mr. John extended a hand, "Name's John."

The man nodded, "The butcher. I know." He shook Mr. John's chubby paw. "I'm Martin. Martin Frobisher."

He said it the way someone says something you're supposed to be impressed by. He said it the way Mr. John talked about prime rib or filet mignon. *Frobisher.* He put so much emphasis on it that Mr. John was instantly annoyed. He hated when he didn't know something. He frowned at the man.

"Frobisher," the floppy-haired man said again.

"Okay?" Mr. John responded.

The floppy-haired man, Martin Frobisher apparently, frowned. He cleared his throat and scrunched up his eyebrows. He studied Mr. John's face to see if the man was messing with him. "I'm of the line of Benjamin Frobisher, founder of the North West Company."

"Ohhh," Mr. John responded, pretending that any of that had meaning to him. "You didn't say you were *that* Frobisher." He still had no idea who this Frobisher was supposed to be. Some of the stuff around town had been stamped with the North West Company when Mr. John was a young man, but he hadn't seen any of that stuff in years. Life must not have been too great for the Frobisher line if they were working as oarsmen in Walla Walla.

The man straightened up his back and tugged on the

collar of his shirt. Mr. John could actually see this kid puffing himself up. *Good Lord, I think I hate this preening kid,* Mr. John thought.

Mr. John kept talking though. "If I know a Frobisher, that's a clan that knows the importance of a buck."

The man, Martin, nodded. "We didn't build the North West Company by being stupid."

We? Mr. John ignored it. "What would you say if I told you I knew where you could get your hands on a nugget of gold the size of your fist?"

Martin chuckled. "I'd say you should quit drinking so fast. That liquor'll go to your head faster than ya think."

Mr. John just nodded. He smiled and waved at the bartender. He hollered at the man behind the bar that he wanted a gill of whiskey. The barkeep showed up at the table, ran a dirty towel over the table as if that made it any cleaner and set down the whiskey. Mr. John made eye contact with the Frobisher kid and smiled. He pulled the ounce of gold out of his pocket and sat it down on the table. Frobisher's eyes spread wide. He stared at the gold the way a hungry man stares at a steak in the butcher shop.

"Keep 'em coming," Mr. John said.

The bartender nodded. "Yessir. Thank you, sir."

He grabbed the gold so fast it seemed like he thought it might vanish back into his imagination. He scurried back behind the bar, never taking his eyes off the gleaming gold.

Frobisher leaned forward. "Okay, I'm listening."

≡≡≡≡≡≡≡

Frobisher ordered another whiskey and Mr. John insisted that the kid put it on his tab. A gill of whiskey was different at just about every bar you went to. They were supposed to be standardized as four ounces, but these shopkeepers had a habit of buying glasses that they thought they could get away with. The one here was even smaller than the one at the Look-See. Just eyeballing it, Mr. John thought the gills were about 3.5 ounces at the Steamed Clam. They cost 10 cents. That didn't seem like much, but he was cheating his customers by 12.5% per gill. In theory, each gill should be about eight or nine cents. Since he was cheating every gill by 12.5%, he could increase his profit by about the same amount. Mr. John didn't have time to gripe about that now. The ounce of gold would pay for about 200 gills. He could buy whiskey for every person in the saloon for the next week probably. That's a good way to get people asking questions, though. In fact, he was already starting to regret flashing his gold so readily. He needed this Frobisher kid to believe him about the gold. That flashy show had definitely done the trick.

The kid motioned for a friend of his to come over. This friend was a bulky, short guy with a face lined and scarred like a fifty year old man. However, he was probably no more than twenty-five. His skin was leathery and tough, like a baseball mitt. There was only one thing that weathered a man like that. This was a man who worked with wild, bucking horses and he was tougher and meaner than any wild horse in the West.

The general store sold a zinc oxide cream that came in a metal tin, but the wrangler didn't like to wear it. It was too dainty and feminine for men of the final American frontier. They didn't want to be soft and pale like their women. Supple, white skin and soft hands were the signs of someone who spent their days under a roof on their butts. They wanted the hard, leathery skin, and the rough, cracked hands that were the signs of a laborer. Mr. John had a callous or two from working a cleaver, but he didn't see any real glory in the weeping blisters that burst on the shoulders of every wrangler as soon as the sun came back for the summer. After a few days of tingling, stinging agony, they tended to adapt, but they were aging quickly. Wranglers were the ones who were most likely to come down with the swelling tumors they called cancer; that seemed to Mr. John a high price to pay to look tough. These hard headed men would be exactly what he needed though.

The man sat down and extended a hand. Shaking his hand was like shaking a rough-hewn boulder. His hands were dry and calloused, laced with muscle and rough skin. "Owen," he said.

Mr. John responded with his own name. He wondered if this rough-cut sack of muscles had a famous name too. If he did, he didn't offer it. The Frobisher kid pointed with his gill of whiskey, drunkenly sloshing whiskey onto the table.

Martin Frobisher said, "The butcher knows where a bunch of gold is."

Frobisher's eyes drunkenly slid away from his buddy to a woman sitting at a table by herself. She wore a dress that bunched at the collar and went high up her neck. She wore a men's coat over her dress. Frobisher's eyes ran down her legs, covered in the light frilly fabric of her dress down to her shoes. Instead of the dramatic pointed toe shoes women wore these days, she was wearing simple leather shoes with flat heels. She wore a massive wide-brimmed hat, though. That was pretty standard for women, but it was more like the kind of hat a cowboy might wear on the range than the hats of women. Honestly, she looked something like an Indian woman. Not in her face very much, but she definitely dressed a lot like the ones Frobisher had seen. He wondered why a nice white lady as pretty as a peach would want to dress like a frumpy Indian.

She was by herself, reading a book -- it was that popular one all the toney highfalutin folks were always talking about, *White Fang* by London. Frobisher had no interest in books, but it seemed like more and more people in Walla Walla were talking about them to try and make it seem like the town wasn't a frontier. If people were reading books in public, well then it had to be a cosmopolitan place. It was nonsense; Frobisher would ignore it for a pretty lady, though.

"What's your name?" He hollered at the woman reading.

She looked up from her book, looked around and finally realized he was probably talking to her. She pointed at her own chest. "Me?"

Frobisher nodded. "I don't see anybody else in here. What's your name?"

"Debbie," she responded, then put her head back in her book.

Annoyed, Frobisher hollered, "Debbie what?"

"Wagner," she said without even looking up from her book.

The boulder-handed man, Owen, grabbed his buddy by the shoulder. "Focus, man."

Frobisher cleared his throat. "Where was I before I was so rudely interrupted?" He took a pause to inhale some whiskey. "Oh yeah, this fat butcher right here -- I don't trust a skinny butcher -- he knows where an injun got a bunch of gold hid."

Over his shoulder, Debbie Wagner's eyebrows ticked up a little bit when she heard him say the word "injun." The very sound of that word grated on her like sandpaper against her throat. She tried to look like she wasn't paying attention to these drunk men, which wasn't very hard. The one they kept calling Frobisher had gotten drunk enough to be hollering. She kept her head in her book, but listened closely.

The butcher leaned forward, putting his elbows on the table. "Youi know that Indian who's always running around here delivering ice?"

"Blackie," Frobisher says.

Owen nods his head. "If I didn't know any better I'd say that boy got some negro in him too."

Mr. John nodded. "Well, that boy come into my shop earlier today to buy some beef shoulder. He plops down this big honking gold nugget. The kind that's all smooth from being right up on the top of the soil."

Frobisher smiles, practically salivating. "Well, where's he keep his gold?"

Mr. John shrugged. "Wherever he lives, I reckon. That's the thing. Nobody knows where this boy lives. I need you fellows to find out where he lives. You're going to need to follow him home tomorrow night. But you have to stay out of sight. If he catches on to being followed, the whole thing's gonna blow up in our faces."

Frobisher patted his hip where he was carrying a pistol, a Colt Single Action Army. The heavy metal pistol jangled against his hip. "If I got to put 'im down?"

Mr. John shrugged again. "Do what you have to do. I can't imagine anybody will miss one savage."

They all laughed and clinked their glasses together. Debbie sipped her beer that had long since gotten warm. The steam beer was room temperature and bitter, the dingy glass sweating into her hand. She closed her book and walked out of the saloon. She vowed never to set foot in the Steamed Clam again. The Look-See was on the other side of town, but if she had to get a drink, she'd go there instead.

═══════════════

The next day, Debbie made sure to get to work a few minutes early. Blackie was always very prompt, and sometimes he was already out on his deliveries by the time she showed up. She needed to make sure she caught him before he went out. She sat at her desk in the ice house, sorting through a list of monthly earnings reports. There were a few places that were over a month behind on their payments. That was to be expected. She did, however, notice that the Steamed Clam was also behind on its payments. She sneered at that. For whatever reason, she had expected that. She'd found that the greedier, more bigoted, and more selfish someone was, the less likely they were to fulfill their obligations -- obligations like paying for their ice on time.

She shifted the Steamed Clam report into the derelict accounts pile on her desk. That pile was growing every day, and it felt like she was never moving a report out of the pile. That was part of life in a place like Walla Walla. The newspapers from New York and Los Angeles could say whatever they wanted about the economy booming and the rise of the progressives in Washington, DC. In Walla Walla, a lot of people were still struggling. That's why the ice house let people buy with lines of credit. A line of credit could be the thing that keeps a struggling saloon in business or keeps a hotel from closing up its restaurant. In fact, the ice house was unique because they even offered lines of credit to negroes and Indians.

Just to the south of the border, black people weren't even allowed to move into Oregon. They were beaten, barred from even traveling into town, and it wasn't uncommon for a black person to get beaten half to death and dropped on the Washington side of the border. It wasn't so bad for negroes in Washington, but you didn't get a complete constitutional ban on negroes in one state without a good amount of hate in all of its neighbors. That's what made the ice house so special; they offered credit to negroes. It wasn't something that a lot of companies did, and it had probably saved several lives. That didn't mean it was popular with the white citizens of Walla Walla, though.

Debbie kept shuffling papers, scratching through various reports and numbers. Her desk was barely in view of the door, so as she moved papers around, she would lean up on her tip toes and look out into the hallway. She'd been at work for about thirty minutes, waiting for Blackie to show up. Every few papers, she looked out into the hallway. She heard the soft patter of footsteps coming down the hall. They sounded like the light, quick steps that signified Blackie. He walked quickly everywhere he went, with short energetic steps. It was almost like he was running everywhere he went, even when he was just walking. Debbie saw him patter down the hallway. His long hair swished in the breeze as he walked. His long braided hair shimmered in the light streaming through the windows.

Debbie jumped to her feet and scurried into the hall. "Blackie," she shouted after him.

The soft-footed man came to a quick halt and spun around. He moved like a dancer, light and graceful on his feet. He smiled at her when he saw her and gave her a quick wave of his hand.

"Hello, Debbie. How have you been?"

She opened her mouth to speak, but then stopped. She didn't know if anyone in the office would be sympathetic to Mr. John and his goons. She grabbed the ice deliverer by his arm and pulled him into her office. Luckily for her, Blackie was an easygoing kind of guy who didn't mind being hauled around by women half his size.

Debbie pulled him into her office and closed the door.

Blackie's eyebrows raised up almost to his hairline. "Um, Debbie?"

"Blackie, someone is going to try to kill you." As soon as she said it, she knew she probably should have phrased it a little bit differently. At least, she shouldn't have closed him into her office before announcing his life was in danger. Judging by the way his mouth dropped open and his eyebrows bunched in the middle of his forehead, he was terrified.

"Wha...?"

She grabbed his shoulders. "Do you have gold?"

He closed his mouth and looked sideways at her, but didn't respond. She was making a mess of this. If he thought someone was going to kill him, why would he ever admit to having a bunch of gold?

Debbie held her hands up in front of her as if she were saying she was unarmed. She took a deep breath that actually lifted her shoulders and dropped them as she exhaled. "Okay, let me start over."

Blackie's eyebrows rose up to his hairline, waiting for something that he assumed was going to be pretty interesting.

Debbie started talking again. "I was at the Steamed Clam last night."

"Alone?" Blackie asked.

The Steamed Clam had a reputation for being something of a rough spot for just about anyone, even the rough hewn farmers and cattlemen who frequented the place for its room temperature whiskey. For a slender woman like Debbie, it could be a death sentence. The way a man reacted in the Steamed Clam could range from hostile to downright dangerous, usually depending on which man she encountered and how much of the house whiskey he'd been drinking. Men, on their soberest of moments, didn't take kindly to being rejected by a woman they felt entitled to. When they were in their cups, they were prone to get violent. Debbie had heard the same kind of incredulity from others when she said she liked to read at the Steamed Clam. They would remark on how dangerous it was to frequent that place, but she would respond by asking where in the world was actually safe for women. It was an unassailable point.

"Yes," She replied, "but that's not important. I was listening to a conversation there. I overheard it really. They were loud, the way people get when they're drunk. Well, the butcher was there."

Blackie's face lit up. A smile touched both ears. "Mr. John? Oh, I like that guy."

Debbie's eyebrows gathered in the middle of her forehead as she looked back with surprise. "Ummm, hmmm, well, he was talking with some other fellows. They seemed like a rough group of guys. They were, um, they were talking about you."

Blackie lifted one eyebrow.

Debbie went on. "The butcher was saying that you paid for some meat with a big hunk of gold."

Blackie shrugged. "Yes, I didn't have a chance to get it changed for cash. The bank closes at dark, and I hadn't had a chance to get there yesterday."

"Well, you overpaid."

"Huh?"

Debbie grabbed Blackie's hand. She didn't know what drove her to do it. If a man had done that to her, she would have seen it as a violation of her personal space, but now that she was talking to Blackie, she felt like they knew each other. They had only seen each other around the office a few times, but they were acquaintances she supposed. They were at the point where they would say "hi" to each other but they didn't really talk. They definitely didn't hold hands. She felt the urge, so she did though. She grabbed his arm and slid down until her hand was resting in his. He looked down at her hand, but didn't move it.

"The butcher stole from you," she said.

Blackie shook his head slowly but he didn't say anything in Mr. John's defense.

She kept talking. "The butcher took more gold than it was actually worth. He stole from you."

"Why would he do that?" Blackie asked, his eyes squinting as if he were trying to literally see what she was trying to say.

Debbie shrugged. "Some people are just rotten, Blackie. But that's not even the point. He was telling people about how he stole from you and you have a bunch of gold, so you had to have gold coming out of a stream on your property. They want your gold, Blackie."

Blackie shook his head. "But it's mine. It's on my land. They can't have it."

Debbie squeezed his hand. He looked down at her hand again. She started to feel awkward about it, so she tried to pull her hand away from his. When he felt her hand starting to slip away, he clamped down on her hand holding it tight. She looked down at it, too. The heat was rising and his hand was starting to slip with sweat, but she didn't want to let go, and apparently, he didn't want her to.

"The way they were talking, Blackie, I don't think they intend to ask about it. I think they're the kind of men who

take what they want. They'll use guns if they have to.
They'll use whatever they want."

"But they don't' even know where I live."

"Exactly." She said, "They're going to try to follow you
home tonight and take your gold."

At that, Blackie burst into a big smile. He threw his
head back and even laughed a little bit. It was Debbie's
turn to be confused. She squinted at Blackie. He took a
deep breath and let it out as a slow, loud sigh.

Blackie said, "Oh, that's a relief."

Her eyes spread as wide as saucers. "What now? It's a
relief they're going to follow you home?"

Blackie smiled and shook his head. "No, they're going to *try* to follow me home." Blackie, not even thinking
about it, lifted her hand to his face and kissed it softly.
"Thank you. You've saved my life. I don't know how I'll
ever repay you."

"Wait, what are you planning?" She asked.

Blackie grinned like a man with a devious plan. "I'm
gonna do my job. Then, I reckon, I'll take the game trail
east to my home."

"How are you going to do that?"

"Well, you see, normally I face north. Then, this is an
old Cayuse trick, I turn to the right." He grinned.

Debbie frowned and stomped her foot. "I'm not amused,
Blackie Sullivan."

That just made him laugh even harder. He experienced something he'd never experienced before in that
moment. He had some experience with women in the past,
and they'd had great times together, but this moment
was something he never experienced before. The closest
he'd ever come was when he fell off a ladder a few years
ago. There was a lull while he was falling. It like he was
standing still and the whole world was actually rushing

upwards past him. He felt like the only point of stability in a world that had lost its mind. Then he hit the ground. It didn't hurt, not at first. Instead, he still felt like he was moving, like the ground was rushing up to meet and trying to drive right through him. But he couldn't breathe. There was nothing but tightness in his chest, but there was no pain. There was just a stillness.

Debbie's pale cheeks turned red with her frustration, as if roses had just bloomed underneath her skin. The red ran up to her eyes. She pursed her lips so they were a little pink line. But when she stomped her foot in anger, her ponytail bobbed on the back of her head. It was the cutest thing Blackie had ever seen. That's when he felt it again. He felt like he was standing perfectly still -- him and Debbie. The rest of the world was rushing around them, but they weren't moving at all. He was a statue -- there was only tightness in his chest and he couldn't breathe. Unlike the ladder, this didn't hurt. This was a tightness, a stress, a gasp that felt welcome. He tried to explain it to himself but couldn't quite figure it out. It was like the moment before a sneeze -- no, that didn't do it justice. That sounded gross. It was like the moment clouds gather on a hot day -- when the sun has been baking Walla Walla for weeks without ceasing. The grass crunches underfoot, the dirt stirs up to cloud with the slightest footsteps, and the wind hasn't moved in so long that the blades of dead grass stand up perfectly straight like dead soldiers. It was like that. The moment when the clouds roll in, but before the rain starts falling. There was a relief to it, but you knew you were only at the tip of the best things to come. It was the moment before something extraordinary.

Debbie crossed her arms. "Is there a reason you're staring at me with your mouth open? You make a very unconvincing fish, Mr. Sullivan."

Was his mouth open? Oh that was embarrassing. He came back to his senses, shutting his mouth. His tongue felt rough and dry as if his mouth had been open for a while. How long had he been staring at her like an idiot?

"Oh, um, sorry," he said. "It's just that, um, I'm pretty fast. I can run fast, I mean."

"So."

"I follow game trails to get home. They won't be able to keep up with me. They're old game trails my dad taught me about. I don't know that anyone knows the Walla Walla Valley as well as I do."

"Some of these trappers around here know the woods pretty well."

Blackie smiled. "I'm sure they do but, Debbie, my father was the last Cayuse Indian. A Cayuse knows this land the way you know your arm or your leg. I could stand right next to you in the forest, and you'd never know it."

"That would be scary."

Blackie shook his head, "No, it wouldn't. You wouldn't know I was there. You couldn't be scared by something you didn't even know existed."

She bit her lip. She looked unconvinced. "You're sure you'll be okay? They can't follow you?"

Blackie nodded. "Not a chance."

She groaned, "Okay, I suppose if you're sure." She agreed to let him go on with his day instead of insisting that he sneak back to his house immediately or hide out with her at her house. He insisted that he could outrun these men and they'd never catch him. She wasn't convinced, though. As much as she didn't want to, she was going to head to the Steamed clam again that night to make sure that they didn't develop some kind of new technique to inflict harm on this man.

He smiled and jogged out of the room. He didn't so

much as run, not the way she had come to understand it. It was more like he unfolded his long legs like an antelope rising to its feet and bounded out of the room. He waved and smiled at her as he moved out of the room. He covered the entire width of the room in about two steps. Debbie shrugged. Well, if that was any indication, then he was pretty fast.

———

The day went by in a pretty unremarkable fashion. The savage who called himself Blackie ran around delivering ice all day. Martin Frobisher and Owen sat around drinking with the butcher, Mr. John. Frobisher talked about how his family had once had a great big fortune, but he didn't actually get to have any of it. He said his name wasn't really Frobisher. His mama and his daddy hadn't been married. Well, that wasn't entirely true. His daddy had been married, but not to his mama, to a respectable woman back home. He'd been traveling through the Walla Walla Valley surveying his new business and he'd taken up with a serving woman while he was in town. He'd left her behind when the train pulled out of the station. Martin liked to believe that his father would have stuck around if only he'd known that the woman was pregnant, but he knew it wasn't true. Who stuck around in the American frontier of thirty years ago who didn't have to? No one.

That's how the frontier got its reputation. It was hard scrabble, barren, and wild. Back East, they talked about the West being "wild" as if that meant it was unregulated. That was a lie. There were laws aplenty and hardhearted lawmen to carry them out. That was the problem, really. There were criminals and there were lawmen, but they weren't much different. It seemed like people tended to slip back and forth from one profession to another. They were just hardhearted men with a taste for whiskey and violence. That's what Martin was. He was in the line of steel nerved men like Wild Bill Hickok, Wyatt Earp, and Johnny Ringo. That's what he told himself at least. He was going to commit this evil act, but then he'd have enough money to go straight. They'd all have enough money. Maybe he'd head on back to Wyoming and get a big ranch full of fat cattle. Hire some Crow or some of the Sioux to work it for him. Now that was a plan. Just the one bad act and then he'd go legitimate. Then again, it was just stealing from an Indian. Who would even really care about that? An Indian didn't know what to do with that kind of money anyway.

He'd known Owen for a while. Owen was another one like Martin Frobisher. He was from Walla Walla. He'd been born and raised in the clutches of the sweltering town. He felt like he had a right to the land, no matter who had been there in the first place. White people had moved in, trampled over every person in their way and erected a town of wood and concrete. In the mind of a white person, that made it yours. To own it, you had to ruin it. That's how you staked your claim. If Martin felt he was in the great tradition of men like Wyatt Earp and Billy the Kid, then Owen was in the great tradition of the conquerors who called them explorers -- the kind of men who moved into an area that already had a name and was covered in people and still insisted that they'd discovered it. He wasn't a modern day Billy the Kid. He felt like Lewis and Clark on their expedition a hundred years ago. He was heading out into the unknown, facing it with blue and green eyes that had never laid upon it before. He was a man who declared himself the master of everything he could see just by virtue of his white skin and the force of his rifles. Black powder and white skin were a deadly combination.

Owen drank beer while Martin drank whiskey. The fat butcher paid for it all. Mostly, he sat around smoking skinny cigarettes and taking the occasional break to hack up phlegm. He was paying for it all. He called it a "down payment" because they were going to get so much gold for him. What he didn't account for was Owen's and Martin's side plan. The two men had to follow the savage up the mountain to wherever he lived and steal his gold somehow. There wasn't much need for a fat butcher in that plan. They didn't reckon he could object overly much if they just cut him out. What was he going to do? Go to the U.S. Marshall and say "I hired two fellas to rob an Indian of his gold fair and square but they cheated me?" Well, he couldn't right do that. So, they figured they were in the clear.

There they sat for most of the day, drinking and watching the street. Women came and went all day while their men were out driving cattle, or dragging ploughs through the dry hardscrabble that passed for dirt out here. Owen and Martin sat around making crude jokes about the different women who went by. In the East, the women wore long dresses that dragged the ground and heavy shoulder pads that ran down to frilly sleeves. Out here, women dressed similarly -- they dressed like Queen Victoria Owen said. The difference was mainly the parasols; they were like umbrellas but instead of being made of anything that could withstand water, they were thin, gauzy affairs. Owen and Martin had been arguing about them for an hour when they finally saw Blackie heading home for the day.

Owen had been making the point that if they were just made of something rain resistant, they would be a lot more useful. Martin was making some kind of point about them being heavy. He was at the point of drunkenness when he couldn't quite keep track of where his thoughts were headed. Hell, he couldn't even remember where he'd started each sentence. They saw Blackie walking by, rubbing a kink out of his shoulder. He was smiling and whistling.

Owen grunted, "What's that savage have to be so damn chipper about?"

Martin slapped his back. "Come on. Let's go ruin his day."

The Butcher ran his bulbous tongue over the adhesive strip on his cigarette paper. He sealed the cigarette and plopped it between his two lips. "Well, get on with it then." He flicked a match off his thumbnail, and it jumped to life. He touched the flame to the cigarette's tip. Smoke immediately started rising from the cigarette.

The butcher blew out a lung of smoke. "Oh, and don't forget who told you 'bout this gold mine."

Owen and Martin nodded and stumbled out the door into the late evening. The sun was starting to fall into the sea, but the temperature hadn't started to slip yet. It was still hot outside -- hot but dry, like opening the door of an oven. They followed Blackie for a while. He walked quickly, like a man with a purpose but didn't act at all like he knew he was being followed. He had long legs and springy steps.

Owen and Martin, heavy with booze, had a hard time keeping up with him without looking conspicuous. An Indian moving through Walla Walla proper was enough of a spectacle for people to notice, but mostly everybody in town knew Blackie so they didn't worry too much about it. However, it was something they noticed. He was exceptionally noticeable because of the long slippery black braid running down his waist and the way he moved. He moved on his long legs like a big cat moved through the jungle.

It was a way that most Indians moved when they were moving through Walla Walla. The white people in town didn't much appreciate having to even see their brown skin; they definitely didn't want to bump into a Native person. So, the natives moved like people stepping through hostile territory. They picked and slipped and squirmed between white people who didn't for half a second consider getting out of the way. It was the way you would slip quietly through a forest. Only, in this jungle, the trees were white people and they were also the vipers.

So, he drew some attention to himself, and two drunk white men stumbling after him would bring some attention as well. To keep their heads down, they started lagging behind.

Owen cleared his throat and said, "We can make up ground after we get past the edge of town."

Martin nodded. His breath was already starting to get caught in his throat. He took a deep breath, trying to catch back up to his breathing. "Damn, this Indian moves fast, don't he?"

After about twenty minutes of following him, Blackie cleared the edge of town and the road gave way to a gravel and dirt track that wound its way into the mountains. It was full dark by the time they got to the edge of town. Once he got a few feet onto the dirt track, Blackie stopped and looked side to side for a second.

Owen and Martin both caught their breath and held it as if their breathing was going to be heard by the Indian. Indians held a semi-mythical status for white people in Walla Walla. No one was quite sure how much they were capable of. Could they hear farther in the forest than white people? Smell better? See better at night? Whatever

the case may be, the night was dark and still. With the air
not moving an inch, sound would carry pretty well. They
didn't risk it. Blackie looked side to side but he didn't look
back.

He dropped down to one knee and adjusted the strap
on his sandals. He rolled his shoulders back and forth to
loosen them up. He straightened up, cocked a leg out and
leaned down to touch the tips of his fingers to his toes.
Owen and Martin realized he was stretching.

Just as soon as Owen could think, "Why is he stretching," Blackie took off. It was something to behold. Martin
had recently seen one of the rich businessmen from the
capital when he visited Walla Walla. The man had been
driving a Studebaker Model C. It was a shimmering, high-
gloss automobile that the people of Walla Walla had only
ever heard of. When the businessman stepped on the ac-
celerator the whole thing shuddered, coiled up, and lum-
bered into action. It was like watching a great beast wake
up from a long slumber. Blackie wasn't like that. Blackie
was like the sled dogs that the Indians up in Canada used
to pull their sleds. They were sitting around, chewing a
bone at one point, and then in the space of one breath, they
could be in full stride, chewing up mileage. It was like
that watching Blackie take off. It wasn't violent. It was
the most natural thing in the world -- a flag unfurling in
the wind, a bullet leaving a gun, an Indian disappearing
into the night

Martin slapped Owen on the back, and they started off
after Blackie. By the time, they realized he was even running, he was already two hundred yards ahead of them.
His footfalls way in the distance were soft like the pitter
patter of rain hitting a gravel road. The two white men's
footfalls were heavy thuds that shook their legs and drove
the force up in to their knees. Their faces jiggled with the

force of their footfalls. They weren't cut out for this kind of travel. They could barely even see.

Blackie could hear the men behind him when he first started running. He had taken the time to stretch, which was good. He'd made the mistake of sitting down after his shift delivering ice. When you spent all day running around, there was really only one thing to be afraid of -- stiffening up. He had been running ice for so long that the work itself didn't bother him. It made him sore and tired, and if he didn't plan properly he would get staggeringly nauseated on occasion. But that was just all about planning when and what he ate. However, there was one thing he could never beat: the chair. After a long day putting miles and miles on his legs, they *wanted* to stop moving. If he let them, they would lock up like seized carriage springs.

So, he had taken a few seconds to stretch his legs back out, which was a good idea. He was in pain, but it was quickly dissipating like working oil into the tracks of a train. They squealed and protested for a while until the oil could completely coat the gears. He was just hitting his stride when the sound of the white men's thundering feet began to disappear. Had he outrun them already? Surely, they were faster than that. He didn't take a chance to glance backwards yet, though. He didn't want them to know that they had been spotted. The way Blackie figured it, if they thought he didn't know they were following him, they would try to catch him again. From the looks of their drunken stumbling, they weren't going to ever be a challenge to outrun. If it meant he had to run home a little quicker each day to avoid being robbed, then he would put up with it.

They would probably lose interest before too long. They didn't seem like the kind of men who had much perseverance in them. Very rarely did someone go from a fine upstanding, hardworking citizen to an armed robber. They would find some easier victim before too long. That was the point of crime: it's supposed to be easier than doing the right thing.

Blackie couldn't hear them anymore and he hadn't heard them for a while. He had barely even gotten to the mountains themselves. The dirt track was just starting to wind up into the wooded area. He took a turn towards his house and glanced backwards. Way back, probably a half-mile behind him, he could just make out two shadows in the night: the two men.

Blackie smirked and put a little extra speed into the next quarter-mile. By that point, he was climbing the mountain towards his house, and the woods had gotten thick enough that they'd never find him. Some robbery attempt, he thought.

He chuckled to himself. The sound of his own voice in the still, hot night was jarring. It sounded so unwelcome in the dark wood. He knew that he was welcome in the wood, though. Maybe it just wanted him to stay silent.

Owen didn't know how long he spent on all fours throwing up into the dirt. Every time he tried to inhale, he felt like his tongue -- dry and swollen thing that it was -- blocked his air passage. He gagged and vomited again. He wanted to get off the ground, but he was a prisoner to the earth. Each shuddering dry heave racked him with pain and shook him to his core. He was heaving so hard that the base of his spine ached.

Martin was already walking back to Walla Walla. He just left Owen in the dirt and vomit.

≡≡≡≡≡≡≡≡≡

Debbie sat down at her usual table at the Steamed Clam. She'd finished *White Fang* earlier that day while she was supposed to be working. It's not that she was a bad employee; she was just a really good reader. She tried her hardest to pay attention but sometimes, it was just so boring. She was worried about Blackie all day long, so eventually she decided that she'd be better off just reading a book. She didn't think she'd get any work done in that state anyway. Well, the book hadn't ended the way that she'd predicted the moment she'd picked it up. When she'd picked it up the man behind the counter at the general store had offered something a little lighter and more "ladylike" for her. He'd said that she would probably have her heart broken by the end.

When she'd asked why, the man had said, "The dog is going to die, ma'am. The dog always dies."

Debbie had shrugged and said, "From what I hear, he's part-wolf. He might surprise you."

The man had shook his head, "Even part-wolf, he's going to die."

Well, the dog hadn't died. In fact, he'd lived and the book had ended with him relaxing in the sun. Maybe one of her favorite aspects of books was the permanence. White Fang had lived through his last encounter, and now he would live forever. Until humanity was swept from the planet, White Fang would be alive. She liked that. In real life, even the best things couldn't last forever.

She had a new book now, though. It was something she'd been waiting almost a year to get in. The man who ordered books for her down at the general store had fought her tooth and nail. He'd claimed they didn't have a supplier. He'd claimed they were sold out. He claimed not to have heard of it. Eventually, after paying triple the normal price, he'd ordered the book for her. The book was *Tuskegee & Its People* by Booker T. Washington. She was excited to get into it. She'd never been to Alabama. In fact, she wasn't even sure she could find it on a map. They'd exterminated the Native Americans in Alabama a long time ago, and they were doing everything in their power to exterminate the black people now. She didn't know what to expect from the book, but one of her pen pals was married to man in Kentucky. She wrote to her about all the horrible things being done to black people in her town. Her husband was one of the men doing the horrible things. That's the way it went. The men were the last to wake up to injustice.

Before she could even open the book, Owen, Martin and the Butcher sat down at a table where they had been the day before. Owen and Martin, the two scruffy drunk men, looked like they'd been rode hard and put away wet. Their hair was plastered to their heads with sweat, their clothes were stained with dirt and mud. One of them, she couldn't remember which one was which, had vomit crusted down the front of his shirt. They smelled worse than horses after a full day on the trail.

The butcher hacked a lungful of phlegm and spat it into the floor. It oozed like crude oil. He took a crooked cigarette out of his shirt pocket, straightened it with his fingers, and lit it with a match.

He was the first to talk. "The hell you mean you lost him?"

Martin shrugged. "The way I figure it, he's the fastest man alive. I ain't never seen nobody move like that."

Owen nodded. "You shoulda seen it. It weren't human. Must be some kind of savage something. You know they run everywhere."

Debbie held the book open like she was reading, but she wasn't. She listened to these men talk about Blackie as if he weren't even human. Listening to them talk made the blood rush to her face. She could feel her heart starting to pump harder, driving blood into her ears and her cheeks. If she could look in a mirror, she knew her face would be bright red. Debbie's mother was a Native; she wasn't quite sure what tribe she'd come from but she knew it was one of the Northwest ones. She didn't have much memory of her mother. She'd been left on the doorstep of a nice missionary family; they were Protestants who believed in converting Native Americans to the Lord. Debbie didn't have much affection for the religion of her adopted parents buts she didn't' have much for her mother's ways either -- whatever they might be.

Despite that Native heritage, Debbie's skin was still pale like old book paper. Her face was scattered with a speckling of freckles across her nose and cheeks like a constellation in the night sky. In fact, despite the fact that she could be considered half-red, she wasn't often actually red. In the summer, her face turned an even tan but even that didn't give away her Native heritage. The only time her skin could be considered actually red was when she was angry or embarrassed and the blood flushed her face. She didn't know much about her parents but she knew that if she hadn't passed for white, her life would be much different. In fact, people would probably talk about her the way these men were talking about Blackie.

They talked about his legs and his calves and his

buttocks as if they were talking about a thoroughbred. They'd been drunk when they'd stumbled into the bar and they were only getting worse. Their words were stringing together like tangled hair, falling all over each other in a sloppy knot.

"I'm tellin' ya," the older one stumbled, "it ain't right. Injuns ain't like us white folks."

The butcher lit a cigarette and shook the match out. He blew out a stream of gray smoke, followed by a hacking wet cough. He eventually hacked up enough mucus that he spat it onto the floor. He wiped his mouth with a damp handkerchief, crusty with old mucus.

The butcher said, "I can't argue with you there. You think you can catch him tomorrow?"

The smaller man, Frobisher, shook his head. "Ain't no catching him. He's like a ghost. We ain't gotta catch him though. We gotta *trap* him."

Owen looked up, cocking a curious eyebrow. "What you mean?"

Frobisher groaned. "We saw where he turned onto the game trail. Alls we gots to do is lay in wait for him on the game trail. When he turns the corner, we put a bullet in his chest and go on about our business. That game trail can only lead to one place."

The butcher tutted his tongue. "What if he doesn't live along the game trail?"

Frobisher shrugged. "He does. Them Indians are always trying to be close to animals. If I didn't know no better, I'd say they was animals themselves."

Owen chuckled. "They are animals. You seen that boy running through the woods. Boy looked half deer I tell ya."

Debbie kept her mouth shut, gritting her teeth. It took everything in her not to say, "He's not half-deer. He's half-wolf."

She kept her mouth shut, though. She was proud of that. She had something of a temper and a habit of running her mouth. It had gotten her more than a few raps across the knuckles when she was younger. Her parents had been missionaries but that didn't mean they were meek or mild. She tried to steady her breathing and hear the particulars of their plans. But, true to their drunken buffoonery, the plan was neither complex nor humane.

Frobisher said, "I'll follow the game trail up about fifty yards or so -- you know, enough to not be seen when he turns up the trail. You hide up in a tree a little ways down, another ten yards or so. When he comes up the trail, you put a bullet in him and then we go about our day."

Owen took a long drink and stared thoughtfully down into the beer. "You know, if we know where he lives, you reckon we need to kill him?"

Frobisher groaned. "You ever panned for gold, Owen? It takes a while. What you reckon that injun'll do if we get caught on his property. He's liable to put some kind of hex on us."

The Butcher blew out a lungful of smoke in a puffy cloud. "Surely, you don't believe that kind of thing."

Frobisher shrugged. "I don't know what I believe. I know them Indians ain't like us. That I know."

Owen chuckled. "That's for damn sure."

The Butcher shrugged. He had a look on his face like he was thinking or like he was constipated. Debbie couldn't quite tell the difference. If she didn't know any better she'd say that he was thinking about what it meant to take an innocent man's life, but that didn't hold with what she'd found of the Butcher. Just when she thought he was about to do something humane, he opened his mouth.

He said, "You boys got guns?"

Frobisher grinned a massive ear to ear grin. It was an

unsettling grin. It was the kind of grin that men got when they were full of whiskey and lust. She knew that look. It was the same kind of smile a hunter got before he pulled the trigger on his prey. Poor Blackie was too good to be prey. Frobisher fished around his waistband and slapped a pistol down on the table with a metallic thud.

Debbie didn't know much about guns, but she'd never seen one like this before. She was expecting a revolver -- big, heavy affairs with a wheel for the bullets. A cylinder, she thought it was called. This didn't have that. It wasn't even as big as the revolvers she was used to seeing on the hips of sheriffs and marshals and frontiersmen. It was a goofy little thing with a set of gears on the side.

The butcher leaned over, picked up the thing and turned it around in his hands. In his meaty paws, it looked like a child's toy.

The Butcher started, "Is that..."

Frobisher said, "A 1901 Mannlicher. Yessir. They make 'em in Austria-Hungary. Semi-automatic. Top of the line."

The Butcher sucked his teeth. "Hmm. You any good with this thing?"

Frobisher nodded. "Oh you'll see."

The butcher gestured at Owen, "What about you? What you got?"

"I got a Spencer repeater I use to put down cattle."

The butcher laughed, choking on smoke. "A spencer repeater? Damn, son, you're in the wrong century. That ain't good for nothing but putting down Confederates."

Owen shrugged and swilled his steam beer. "I reckon an Indian dies just as easy as a rebel. Don't you?"

The Butcher shrugged. "I suppose so. Before my time, but my Daddy used to tell me that one Confederate was as good as any ten Yankees."

Frobisher grinned. "Damn shame they were outnumbered ten to one then wasn't it?"

The butcher laughed. "I reckon so." He took a breath, then said, "You any good with that Spencer?"

Owen nodded. "Blackie's gonna be dead by this time tomorrow."

Debbie closed her book -- in fact, she slammed it closed. She didn't even bother if they heard her. She noisily slid her chair backwards, the legs scraping against the wood. She stood up and walked out. Her lip curled up towards her nose as if she smelled something disgusting.

———

Blackie walked into the Look-See. The air was thick with cigar and pipe smoke. The two flavors, distinct from each other, melded to create the easily-distinguished smell of the Look-See. It was mostly empty in there except for a few people. Blackie recognized most of them.

He recognized King Roger -- a goofy fellow who pretended to be descended from English royalty. Blackie wasn't so sure if he was pretending or if he really thought that he was descended from the royal line. Either way, it was odd. America fought two wars to get free of the British.

King Roger nodded to Blackie and Blackie nodded back. Roger was sitting with the farmer named Buddy. Buddy was a man of only a few words but he loved his whiskey. Blackie had never heard him have a cross word for anyone.

Buddy waved at Blackie, "Hot one out there, eh Blackie?"

Blackie smiled. "It's not quite as hot with fifty pounds of ice on your back."

Buddy sipped his whiskey. "In that case, I'll see you bright and early tomorrow morning for my shift."

Blackie grinned. "Who will milk your cows?"

Buddy sipped his whiskey. "That's true. Maybe next week, then."

"Sure thing."

It was almost the exact conversation they always had whenever Blackie went into the Look-See. Buddy would comment on how hot it was or how rainy or how dry or anything else that he'd observed. Blackie would say how it was better with a bunch of ice on your back. Buddy would promise to join Blackie until someone reminded him of his farming obligations. Blackie didn't remember how it had gotten to that point, but he thought that it was probably a legitimate conversation they'd had a few years ago when Buddy had been drunk and genuinely forgotten that he had farming obligations.

Blackie leaned up against the bar. Looking Glass was wiping down a beer mug with a rag. The rag was probably as dirty as the beer mug, so it was something of a futile exercise. Habits, Blackie guessed.

Looking Glass set a mug down. "Beer?"

Blackie shook his head. "No, not today. I, umm, I need your help."

Looking Glass noticed the concerned look on Blackie's face. His eyebrows were bunched up in the middle of his forehead. "What's wrong, Blackie?"

"I need that," Blackie said and pointed. Looking Glass followed Blackie's finger with his eyes. Blackie was pointing at the rifle with the engraving of the Lewis and Clark expedition on it.

"The rifle?" Looking Glass asked. His eyes slid back to Blackie Sullivan. Blackie could see fear written all over the face of Looking Glass.

Blackie nodded.

"What for?" Looking Glass asked.

Blackie leaned forward, lowering his voice. "How long have you known me, Looking Glass?"

"A couple years," the man said.

"Okay, and have you ever known me to be a man who gets angry? Or who gets drunk and flies off the handle?"

Looking Glass responded, "I can't say I have."

"Well, then do you trust that I'll use this rifle in a way that is responsible? Do it the way I have to do it and not do nothing else?"

Looking Glass thought about it for a little while. He took a deep breath. He looked back over his shoulder at the newly-polished rifle gleaming in the lamp light. He let his breath out slowly. He looked back at Blackie.

He turned around, stepped up onto his toes and lifted the rifle off the hook. He held it the way one holds a baby, careful and gentle. Eventually, he held it out at arm's length.

"Here, don't do nothing stupid."

Blackie took the rifle from Looking Glass. "I'll bring it back. I promise."

Looking Glass patted Blackie on the shoulder, "Don't kill nobody that don't need killing."

V

1847

The Cayuse were naturally wary of Marcus Whitman and his wife, Narcissa. The Cayuse, as a rule, didn't trust white people. Marcus felt that it was a little bit unfair. Sure there had been some people, some white settlers, who had mistreated the Natives in some way or another. There were a few settlers, especially those around Arizona and the Dakotas who gave the local Indians smallpox on purpose. They gave them the smallpox blankets, but that wasn't very common. For the most part, the white people -- at least to Marcus Whitman's mind -- had been more than gracious to the Native Americans.

The way Marcus saw it, there were only a few Natives in the entire country but they wanted the whole damn thing. As far as Marcus could tell, they were always going on and on about how no one could actually own the land, but when white people put up fences, they acted like white people had no claim to it.

There in the silvery blue moonlight, Marcus chuckled to himself. Natives could complain about white people and their fences all they wanted, but they didn't have the numbers or the guns. Nobody cared about the anger of an unarmed man. That wasn't the only thing they complained about either. The local Cayuse who lived on the other side of the wood from Narcissa and Marcus complained nonstop about his use of pesticides and wolf poison. They talked about achieving a balance with the earth so that you could live in harmony. Well, the damn wolves were eating his chickens, and the bugs were chewing his watermelons down to the vines, so apparently harmony was out the window.

By the silver of the moon, Marcus Whitman tiptoed through his watermelon patch with a heavy paper bag of strychnine under his arm. The bag, probably about twenty pounds, tipped over and sprinkled powdery poison over the rows of melons as he walked between the rows. Marcus had a suspicion that the Natives didn't give a damn about harmony with the earth; they just wanted to steal his watermelons -- if he used poison on them then they couldn't steal them and eat them. So, they made up some kind of religious mumbo jumbo that conveniently favored them eating free food.

Well he'd worked too hard to let bugs, wolves, or Cayuse eat his crops. He emptied the entire bag of poison between the rows.

Now, for the wolves. He reached into the sealed leather bag hanging around his hip. The bag was a leather hip satchel that had been sealed with a coating of pig fat to make it waterproof. In the bag, he carried hunks of pig meat -- feet and jowls mostly. In the South, they were the cuts of meat you tossed out to your slaves. He didn't have slaves in Oregon, but he did have wolves. The meat had been soaked in a strychnine solution for the whole day. The wolves didn't much care for watermelons but they couldn't resist the fatty cuts of pig meat.

He chuckled and whispered to himself, "Good enough for negroes and wolves alike."

Around the edge of his melon patch, he tossed the poisoned meat past the tree line. Almost on cue, he heard wolves howling into the night sky. He had about fifteen pounds of pig meat to spread around. The pig had been rooting around in the pig pen earlier that week. It was still fresh -- not that wolves cared much about that.

The morning came, signaled by the roosters the way it was every morning. That was one of the biggest lies that anyone told. Out in the country, the people tended to say that the rooster signals the morning. In fact, the rooster signals the very first hint of light, which is about two hours before the sun ever actually makes its way into the sky. It's not as useful as Marcus had told Narcissa they would be. She didn't have much desire or much reason to be up that early in the morning. But once the roosters started crowing, she couldn't get back to sleep. For whatever reason, Marcus could sleep right through the hollering of the roosters, but she wasn't quite as good at it as he was.

She was from Prattsburgh, which wasn't exactly the brightest and most cosmopolitan part of New York, but this was something entirely different. She was probably, as far as she could tell, the only white woman on this side of the Mississippi River. When they'd first gotten to Oregon, she'd been scared that everything she'd heard about the natives in the West had been true, but she'd found that the Native Americans she encountered were people just like her and Marcus. They had similar ambitions, fears, and dreams. She even spent a good amount of her time living with the Cayuse women. They had danced around each other very cautiously at first, considering carefully how much to share with each person. However, as time went on, they grew more comfortable. The women had the same concerns as any other mothers, sisters, and wives. They wanted good things for their children and their husbands. They worried about the local economy and the harvest yield.

They were different in a lot of ways, too. But their differences really felt like surface issues. The Natives had a respect and a reverence for dirt and trees more than any white woman would probably ever understand. The way Narcissa saw it, the earth and all the items on it were there for humans to utilize. That's what the bible said and that's what she believed. All the beasts of the earth, birds of the air, and fish of the sea were for humanity's edification. The natives felt differently, but they weren't honestly so different.

As she normally did when the roosters got so loud that she couldn't sleep, Narcissa slipped out of bed. She slipped a warm robe around her shoulders. She considered putting on a pair of shoes but the weather had been pretty nice overnight. The ground would still be dry and warm. She walked out the door of their house and into the grassy lawn. The grass tickled between her toes.

The air had a chill to it that felt damp and heavy, the way it normally felt during the moment. The sun was just barely starting to peek over the hills to the east. It was bringing with it a palpable heat, but it would be an hour or so before it actually got warm out. The ground was still warm though; it held onto the sun's legacy longer than the outside air. She headed around to the back of the house where the crops should be growing vigorously in preparation for summer. Marcus would probably have to hire a native to help him pull up some of these vegetables before the sun or the wolves got to them. Some of the crops like watermelons could survive, but the tomatoes would wilt in the summer heat. Also, the birds would get bold once the vegetables ripened.

Narcissa padded barefoot into the backyard to check on the garden. She didn't understand what she found. She found the melon patch picked clean. It was as if her husband had harvested the entire melon patch overnight. The vines, spreading all over the garden like the intricate arteries of the garden itself were completely bare. Just yesterday they had been swelling with massive watermelons that easily weighed ten pounds each. Now, they were completely barren. The only indication that watermelon had ever been there were the depressions in the damp dirt where the watermelons had been. They were like little craters.

Narcissa put a surprised hand over her mouth. She'd never seen anything like this before. Who would do this? She stepped closer to the watermelon patch and noticed that there were footsteps all over. They were the smooth soled shoes the Cayuse normally wear -- Narcissa was no tracker by any stretch of the imagination but she had some of those same shoes made by some Cayuse women as a gift. She knelt down and inspected the footprints. They were clear in the drying ground. Why would the Cayuse do this? This wasn't even how the Cayuse would do it. The women would tell Narcissa about some times when their husbands would steal the horses of a rival tribe. They would show up under cover of darkness, remove all the horses, and not a leave a trace that they'd ever existed in the first place. This was different though. They'd left footprints everywhere, even showing the direction they had left the patch. They had hacked the watermelons off the vines with sloppy hacks. Some of the hacking had actually severed the vines.

Her first instinct was that this was the work of some drunken Cayuse who were up to no good, but she didn't know drunk people to ever be very quiet. If they had in fact been drunk people, then they would surely have woken her up with their stage whispering and their stumbling. No, this was the work of someone who wanted it to be obvious that it was the Cayuse and obvious that they weren't wolves. This wasn't the work of animals; it was the deliberate work of the Cayuse from nearby. They wanted Marcus and Narcissa to know that.

Narcissa instantly knew why. They'd had a dispute with the Cayuse for years now. Marcus insisted on his fences. He insisted on US dollars for his produce when the Cayuse wanted to trade. He'd tried to drag the Cayuse kicking and screaming into the 19th century, but they insisted on acting as if they weren't in the United States. Looks like it boiled over.

Narcissa took a deep breath and whispered to herself, "Let this be the end of it."

Those watermelons would have brought them a little bit of money and she did love a cold watermelon on a hot day, but if this was as bad as the disagreement got, she could live with that. She went inside to wake up Marcus and tell him what had happened to his watermelons. Then she decided against it. Better just to let him sleep. It was going to be a long day.

The knock at the door came sometime around the height of the day. The knock was rapid and frantic. Boom. Boom. Boom. It was the kind of side-of-the-fist knocking that sheriffs and marshals were known for. Marcus looked up from the book he was reading. He was reading *Poor Folk* by a Russian named Fyodor Dostoevsky. Narcissa didn't care for the foreign writers as much as Marcus.

He set down his book, making sure to slip a strip of paper to hold his page. He went to the door and opened it.

The door crashed open and a Cayuse man collapsed into Marcus. He caught the man and dragged his lifeless body into the room.

"Oh my," Narcissa shouted.

"Help me get him to the kitchen," Marcus shouted to Narcissa.

The kitchen was where he did most of his doctor work. With her help, he was able to get the man's seemingly lifeless body to the kitchen. They dragged the man up onto the kitchen table just as soon as he started convulsing. Marcus pulled the man's eyelids open. His eyes were dilated and milky. They weren't seeing a thing. Marcus knew what was happening. He recognized strychnine poisoning when he saw it. The man convulsed and shook.

"What's wrong with him?" Narcissa asked.

Marcus pulls a chair out and sits down at the kitchen table. He crosses one leg over the other and chews on his lip.

"Dear, do we have any of those tea cakes remaining? Those were delicious."

Narcissa's eyes spread wide. "What?"

"The tea cakes, dear. The ones from yesterday."

Narcissa screamed, "A man is dying, Marcus."

Marcus studied the shaking man trembling on the kitchen table. "Him? No, he's fine. Just a little strychnine poisoning."

Narcissa grabbed Marcus's shoulder, "How would you know he's suffering from strychnine poisoning?"

"I put out strychnine. Stands to reason it poisoned him."

"Aren't you going to help him?" She asked.

Marcus shrugged. "He comes to our house overnight and steals our food. Our food. Now, when it goes badly for him, he suddenly wants our help. When it comes to our food, our land, and our god, they hate the white man and his ways. Ohhh, but now that he needs help, he's more than happy to ask for the white man's medicine."

Narcissa leaned against the wall. She'd heard her husband talking about Native Americans in the past. He had something of a bad taste in his mouth for them and their different customs, but she'd never seen him abandon his duties as a doctor. What was it that oath said? The first rule of a physician was to do no harm.

She spat at him, "What happened to 'do no harm'?"

He shrugged. "I didn't do the harm. I imagine that was the poison."

There was a knock on the door again. It wasn't as frantic as the first knocking, but it still seemed like it was someone who was in a hurry. Narcissa groaned at the callousness of her husband and went to answer the door. She opened the door and saw a Cayuse woman doubled over in pain. The woman had one hand on the doorframe and one hand on her stomach. She groaned quietly as the pain hit her in waves.

"Something's wrong," the woman moaned.

Narcissa felt she recognized this woman. She couldn't quite place it. It wasn't a woman who was normally at her meetings with the other Cayuse women, but she had seen her around town. What was her name? She was pretty she knew it.

Narcissa put her hand on the woman's shoulder, "White River. What's wrong?"

The woman's shoulder was hot like she'd been standing

in the sun for hours. She was sweating through her shirt and down her forehead. It wasn't that hot outside. This heat had to be coming from inside her.

"You're burning up," Narcissa said.

White River nodded. "Bad melons. It was the melons."

"It could have been the meat," Marcus said, chuckling from behind his wife.

Narcissa spun around to see her husband smiling and laughing. He looked like a child who had been given a chance to eat a piece of candy.

Marcus smirked, "I warned you injuns about poisoned meat. Left it out for the wolves. Looks like you found it."

White River collapsed, her chin hitting the steps of the porch. The force slammed her mouth shut on her tongue. She spat a mouthful of blood that dribbled down her chin.

Marcus whistled. "Whooo, looks like that one's gonna die. Must be because she's smaller than the man. Pity."

Narcissa shouted at Marcus. "Help her."

For a few more days, Cayuse folks were coming up to the house in a steady stream. It was probably about a dozen or so in all. Marcus eventually started treating them. He gave most of them pills, but he gave a few of them actual injections.

After they were treated, most of them actually started feeling worse and not better. They were complaining about feeling weak and dizzy. Several Cayuse were collapsing while they were working. One man, a trapper, actually died while tracking a deer through the woods. Many of them complained of seizures that would grip them suddenly and render them incapable of moving. A few fell asleep and died in their sleep.

The Cayuse around town started accusing Marcus Whitman of poisoning them. One of the Cayuse who had actually studied with a doctor in Salem, Oregon recognized the symptoms. He accused Marcus of poisoning the Cayuse with cyanide after he'd already poisoned them with strychnine. Obviously, Marcus denied all of the allegations. That was a lie.

━━━━━━━━━━━

Joe Lewis had a rifle, and he knew how to use it. He'd spent some time in the Iroquois Confederacy and been educated in Maine, but he'd learned everything he needed to know traveling through the untamed territories the white people insisted on calling Louisiana. He was half-black and half-Iroquois. Every part of him was hated in just about every corner of North America and he felt that truth like a weight on his shoulders. Every morning, he woke up, put on his clothes and put on the yoke of oppression. No matter what he did, he was never going to stop being Negro and Iroquois. It's hard to stress how deeply that kind of pain drove Joseph Lewis. The hatred of white men everywhere he went was a force that was almost physical. He could feel the hate they had for him. It rotted like bad meat in his guts. It stole sleep from him, battered his will, and drove him to drink.

In addition to his gun, Joe Lewis had a rosary. He was a man devoted to the Catholicism that had taken hold across the Southern part of the country. The Mexican influence on much of the Southwest made Catholicism a pretty routine part of life in those parts, but when he left, he found a new bigotry. People hated him for being Negro. They hated him for being Iroquois. They also hated him for being Catholic. They called him a papist. He couldn't imagine what was so bad about being devoted to the Lord's emissary on earth, but these supposed Christians were so mad at him for not being the right kind of Christian. They wanted him to be something he wasn't. Perhaps that could summarize Joe Lewis' entire life up to that point -- white Americans wanted him to be something that he wasn't. Something he couldn't be. In response, he grew more devoted to the Pope, to the one true religion of the world, and his rifle. He was very loyal to his rifle. He prayed to it as much as he prayed over his rosary beads. In the frontier of Oregon, a rosary was a comfort -- it was comfort that the Lord of the universe would one day welcome him as a friend. The rifle was immediate comfort. The rosary might help him for eternity; the rifle helped him now.

Joe kept the rifle across the back of his shoulders with his hands hanging on it. He was trying to look relaxed, but in reality, he looked like a man who was losing his grip on the world around him. He was red-faced and angry, spitting and cursing, and sweating as he hollered into the crowd of people around him. The crowd of Cayuse and a couple of other Native Americans had gathered around Joe Lewis the longer he talked. He was something of a minor celebrity in Walla Walla due to his rifle. He never told anybody where he got it, but it was supposedly a rifle that Lewis and/or Clark had carried on that first expedition to conquer the Louisiana territory. There were some who doubted that it was authentically a Lewis or Clark rifle. How could you verify something like that? However, it did have a beautiful filigreed engraving of an expedition on the receiver. It was a flintlock, though. By that point in 1847 most people had converted their flintlocks to a caplock or they'd bought a whole new rifle altogether. Not Joe Lewis, though. He kept the rifle in the original flintlock from the late 1700s, early 1800s. It definitely could be a rifle from 1804. People came to see it. That's why Joe Lewis brought it out whenever he wanted to get to rabble rousing. If he was in a particularly good mood after hollering about the white man, he would let the townspeople pass around the rifle and look at a piece of American history. In a way, it was kind of the beginning of American history in that part of the world.

They listened to the dark-skinned Native man holler for the better part of an hour.

"And that supposed doctor," he shouted, "Marcus Whitman. He ain't no doctor I ever heard of. They got all them fancy words that are supposed to mean they better than us. The white man is always saying he's better than we are. They say, don't do things the way your ancestors did. They say their medicine is better than the medicine that the earth has provided for us since the beginning of time."

He gestured with the rifle as if shooting into the air.

"And look what comes of their medicines. You ate the watermelons that came from the earth, but you got sick. Why did you get sick? Has the earth ever poisoned you in this way before? No. Never. The earth provides. It is the white man that poisons the earth. Marcus Whitman, who claims to be a man of God, poisoned the melons to hurt Natives." He was getting increasingly angry and worked up. He was starting to feed off the crowd that was starting to nod along.

"How dare he come here and poison our earth? We are an original peoples. Look at us. The Cayuse, the Illini, the Iroquois. The Nez Perce and the Creek. We all look the same. We're an original peoples. Have you ever had the sunburn your skin? Have you? No. Because we are an original peoples. The white man comes in every shade of the earth, because he is not original. And look at him, burned by the sun. When the sun burns his skin, he almost looks like a Native. He almost looks like an original people. But this man, he poisons the earth for his own gain."

The people by now were hollering and shouting. They were fully in agreement with Joe Lewis. He had them. But he wasn't done riling them up. He was loving their anger too much.

He went on, his volume getting louder. "When you go to him to right his wrong. When you go to him for his white man's medicine, he gives you medicine that doesn't make you better. It makes you worse. It's not bad enough that he poisoned you the first time. When you go to him to fix his wrong, he poisons you a second time. What kind of creature does this? Does a viper bite its victim twice? Does a wasp sting you twice? You or you? Have you ever killed a buffalo more than once? Only when the first shot does not kill it. That's what we have here, folks. He tried to kill you with poison in his melons. When that didn't kill you, he poisoned you again. He wants you dead."

The crowd was screaming now. They were shouting at him. They were teeming like a hive of hornets that had just been kicked. Now was the time to drive it home.

He took a deep breath and boomed, "Well, I want him dead. What do you say? It's time to return the favor to Marcus Whitman."

Things started happening faster than even Joe Lewis had planned for them. He marched off his soap box and tucked his rifle under his arm as if he were ready to shoot the next person who stepped in front of him. He walked down the dirty dust road. He didn't even wait to see if anyone would follow him; he had to project strength. A leader didn't wait for anyone to follow him; he demanded that they follow him. He brought, by sheer force of right and by his example, the confidence that they were about the Lord's work. He was worried though that no one would follow him. If he didn't have any followers, he wasn't much a leader. An old joke said that a leader who didn't have a following was just a man taking a walk. A war band leader who didn't have a following was just a man taking a walk to his death.

Joe Lewis didn't plan to die here in Oregon. He was a man of the East and he wanted to return to it before he died. He would, though, if he had to. He'd die in the hard Oregon dirt. He'd return himself to the earth from which he'd come and not be sad about it. The earth would embrace one of its own, an Iroquois. And God himself would embrace one of His own, a Catholic. He wasn't going to die though. With his rosary in his pocket and a 50 caliber minie ball in his rifle, he was never going to die. Not while the Lord God wanted him alive.

He was emboldened when he heard the people behind him, though. He was sure the Lord God would provide but he also had to admit that having a crowd of Cayuse behind him was going to make him feel a lot better. He didn't dare look back at them for fear that his uncertainty would show in his face, but he had to guess that it was at least two dozen people. A cloud of dust rose everywhere they went down the dusty road. They headed straight for the Marcus Whitman house.

The banging on the door shook Marcus out of his reverie. He was sitting at his kitchen table with a cool rag on the back of his neck and a cold tea in his hand. He heard the frantic knocking at the door. It had to be another one of those Indians whining about stomach cramps and poisoned food. They didn't know it would probably pass in a day or two. They didn't know much about Western medicine, so how would they know this? He thought about just letting this one pass out right on his porch. He kept knocking though.

Whitman jingled his ice in the cup. Finding ice out on this roughhewn frontier was no easy task. Indians ran it all over the country on their backs. He couldn't really plan on when he was going to get another shipment of ice. It was incredibly expensive and he was watching it melt in his iced tea. The Indian kept banging on the door.

Marcus groaned, "Fine."

He stood up and walked towards the door. He kept his iced tea in his hands, though. He wasn't about to lose the last bit of ice because some Indian thought he should eat stolen food. He yanked the door open but was confused by what he saw.

It wasn't an Indian at all. It was some skinny straw-haired white kid. This kid couldn't be more than 16 years old and 110 pounds. He had floppy hair pressed to his forehead with sweat. He pushed the sweat out of his eyes.

"Mr. Whitman. Mr. Whitman, sir."

"What?" Marcus replied.

There were other white people behind him. There were about a dozen white people spread out in front of his house. They were carrying rifles and pitchforks. Marcus's first thought was that they had come for him because he'd poisoned the Indians. That couldn't be, though. There were at least fifteen people here and he didn't imagine you could find fifteen people willing to kill a white man on behalf of some Indians. So, what exactly could this be about?

He looked at the different people who were gathered. He recognized some of them. He recognized the red-faced white man with the big barreled shotgun under his arm. It was the old kind of shotgun that many people still called a blunderbuss. It was a caplock shotgun that you shoved a fistful a lead and a plug of gunpowder into. They were devastating. Many people called them street sweepers, and that seemed like a more apt name. Marcus really hoped they weren't here to kill him.

That street sweeper could put a hole in his body that was big enough to see through. If he'd packed his shotgun with something more devastating like a slug, the hole would be even bigger. It would probably slam him back into his own house. He'd get shot on the porch and die in the hallway. He'd heard a story once about a guy who had reloaded his shotgun with a roll of quarters. The story is different depending on who told it -- some said it was a roll of quarters and others said it was just a few quarters. Whatever it was, it had ripped a man to shreds. That's what those guns did. Now Marcus Whitman was locking eyes with a man carrying one.

"What you going to do with that smoke wagon, friend?"

The man looked down at it then back up at Marcus. "The name's Bewley. Crocket Bewley."

"That's a mighty fine name, Mr. Bewley."

Crockett shrugged. "Heard there was some Injuns coming to kill you and yours. Reckoned we'd help you out."

Marcus let out a long sigh that couldn't express how relieved he was. He was only relieved for a second, though. Then he realized the implications of what the man had said.

"Indians coming to kill me?"

Bewley nodded. "It would seem they think you poisoned 'em. That a fact?"

Marcus shrugged. "I suppose it is."

Bewley smiled. His smile grew bigger and bigger until he broke into laughter. He laughed so hard that his shoulders bounced up and down. "Oh, Lord in heaven,

I woulda liked to see that. I bet them injuns was quite a-bellyaching. Oh, I bet they was."

The other men in the group started laughing. Marcus looked around. It was the best of America gathered here on his yard. It was a group of white men armed with big guns and strong resolve. That's the America Whitman had been promised when he was just a boy. The Founding Fathers had prescribed that keeping and bearing arms was needed for the maintenance of a free state. He looked around at all these men bearing arms and thought that the Founders had been infinitely wise. Had they known that the white man would expand westward and face a growing Indian menace? They must have because the only thing that saved a white man from a savage was a steady hand and a big gun. Luckily, he had a bunch of men with both.

Marcus held his hands up and addressed the crowd of men around him. "Well, gentleman." At that moment, Narcissa walked out and interrupted his speech.

Marcus looked to his wife and shooed her away. "Go inside, honey. Trouble's coming. Don't come out, no matter what you hear."

Narcissa covered her mouth. "Trouble? What kind of trouble?"

Marcus hissed at her. "Just go inside."

She threw up her hands and stomped aside. She slammed the door behind herself too. She slammed it so hard that the wall shook.

Marcus shook his head and turned back to the crowd of men with firearms. He held up his hands. "Listen, gentlemen. I appreciate you coming here. Let me say to you, this country is a country by, of, and for white men. No savage will ever..."

The blood burst out of his mouth and dribbled down his

chin. He tried to speak but only bubbled with the sound of air and blood. He felt the pain like a burning stain on the back of his shirt. It felt like someone pressed a hot iron to his back and left it. He groaned, blood bubbling in his throat. He reached around to his back and felt the gleaming edge of a hatchet, buried between his shoulders. He tried to breathe but inhaled only needles and fire. He looked around at the men standing around; they looked like they were in shock. None of them moved. None reached for a gun. In fact, they probably hadn't even seen the hatchet. They looked thoroughly confused.

With a straining reach, Marcus got his hands around the handle of the hatchet. He knew he shouldn't but he yanked it out. The pain instantly disappeared. Then, like waves crashing against the rocks, the pain doubled, and tripled. Hitting him with such intensity that he dropped to his knees. The blood rushed down his back like a hot, sticky river. The thick syrup glued his shirt to his back. He felt the world rock and his head swim. Stars swam across his vision. He collapsed, smashing his face into the ground.

He slipped into the blackness. The men around suddenly realized what was happening as the blood seeped into the dirt around Marcus Whitman.

Bewley shouted. "The Indians are here." The men started scrambling, pulling pistols from their waistbands or holsters. They shouldered rifles and spun around, looking for the Native Americans hiding somewhere. Instead, they ended up just sweeping their guns back and forth, pointing them at each other or at the trees more than anything else.

"Where the hell are they?" Bewley shouted.

Joe Lewis stepped out of the woods with this rifle on his shoulder and his eye to the sights. He had his sights on

Bewley, the metal post and notched sight cradled the red-faced Bewley. Joe Lewis stepped forward with his cheek pressed to the stock of the rifle.

"Hey there," Joe Lewis shouted, "do you have any last words? Would you care that I perform last rites?"

Bewley swung around his shotgun and brought it up to his shoulder to squeeze off the barrel of hot lead. Joe Lewis was faster though. Joe Lewis's rifle -- the one supposedly carried by Lewis and/or Clark -- barked hot fire. Fire and metal sprayed out of the barrel followed by a cloud of dense black smoke. The 50 caliber miniball hit Bewley in the chest at about 800 feet per second. It was fast enough to punch a hole into Bewley's chest and burst out of his back. The hole went straight through the left side of his chest, throwing him backwards like a punch to the heart. The decompression in Bewley's chest was so quick that he was dead before he hit the ground. By the time he hit the ground, his heart had stopped beating and had drained all of its blood into the dirt.

Joe Lewis dropped the rifle into the dirt and reached into his waistband. He pulled a hatchet out of his waistband in his left hand. In his right hand, he produced a Kentucky pistol. The Kentucky pistol was popular a few years earlier. He preferred them to some of the newer models; they were lethal machines of brutal efficiency. They weren't very good at doing much but shooting a lead ball in a straight line, but he liked the ability to pack as much powder as he wanted in each shot. In fact, he had a habit of over packing his pistol with powder. It robbed him of a little bit of accuracy but at the distances he wanted it for, it wasn't much of a sacrifice. He needed a pistol to put a man down at a short distance. That was more important than accuracy.

There was a strange moment of peace in the middle of

the madness. Bewley was bleeding into the dirt, already in the middle of a meeting with the Lord of Heaven and Earth. Marcus Whitman was rasping and groaning as the gaping wound in his back wept blood into the mud. There was peace in that moment, though. Joe Lewis looked up from the bloody mess that had been Bewley and the other white men just looked back him. He gripped his Kentucky pistol tight enough that his knuckles turned white and he was sweating into the handle. He was so sweaty and gripping so tight that the wood actually groaned under the stress. He could hear himself breathing. He thought he would be stressed but he had never felt more calm in his entire life. It seemed Joe Lewis had found his calling. He was a man who lived by the feud and righteous killing animated him. He felt like he could see more clearly and hear more clearly than he ever had in the past.

He followed the eyes of one white man down to that man's pistol. His hand was hovering over the handle of a pistol. It was an 1847 Colt Walker. It was a new kind of revolver -- very powerful and very expensive. It was designed by a man named Walker who had been out in Texas and couldn't kill as many Mexicans and Indians as he felt he should. So he made a new type of gun. Joe Lewis decided at that moment to take that man's gun -- a gun designed to kill Indians in the hands of an Indian. It would be poetic.

Joe Lewis, in a voice calmer than he thought possible, said, "You move a muscle and I'll drop you."

The man didn't say a word and didn't move a muscle. Before he could make his decision, a dozen screaming Cayuse came flying out of the woods. They streaked forward, hollering and whooping. A man in the front -- Joe Lewis didn't remember his name -- leveled a rifle and pulled the trigger. It was an old style flintlock rifle. A puff of smoke shot straight up in the air before the rifle boomed and the barrel vomited smoke and steel. The lead ball hit the man with the Walker Colt in the forehead. The man dropped to the ground with the top of his head missing.

Joe Lewis had just enough time to express regret that he hadn't made the kill and now it wouldn't be right to take the man's pistol. As soon as he had that thought, he steadied his pistol on the closest white man he could find. Then, hell fell on earth. Years later, some of the people who were there would testify before the court and they would say that everything happened incredibly quickly. Joe Lewis didn't doubt that things had happened really quickly for them. It was a chaos of thundering weapons, black gunpowder smoke, and fountains of blood. It wasn't happening quickly for Joe Lewis.

He felt almost like he wasn't even himself. He felt like someone who was looking down at Joe Lewis. He could see the entire battlefield -- that's what it was, a battlefield, even if only about two dozen people were fighting. They were close enough that Joe Lewis extended his arm and pulled the trigger of his Kentucky pistol. The gun belched smoke and fire. He was so close to the white man that the spraying embers of gunpowder hit the man's shirt and kindled. He flailed backwards, slapping at the flames on his shirt and not even paying attention to the hole in his chest. That is, until he finally lost enough blood that he passed out. He let out a final gasp and went silent.

Joe Lewis dropped the pistol into the dirt. He could pick it up after they'd finished killing the white men. They were all richer than he could ever dream of being and they had nicer guns than he would ever be able to afford. Maybe he'd just steal a bunch of guns from these white men. That was for later though. Right now he was most concerned with the weapons in his hands. He only had the one and it was a hatchet. Bullets were flying in every direction. He felt like he could actually see the bullets and miniballs, but that was obviously impossible. Whatever the case, he was seeing so clearly and so quickly that he felt like he could see straight through the fog.

Through the fog, he spotted a white man shoot a cap-lock rifle. He dropped the rifle and reached for his pistols. In that moment, Joe Lewis flung his hatchet through the fog. It disappeared into the world of shadow but then froze in mid-air. It hovered in the middle of the air, attached to the head of the man on the other side of the fog. Then the man and the hatchet disappeared to the ground.

Then Joe Lewis was somewhere he hadn't planned to be. He was standing in the middle of an active massacre without weapons. He looked around him and saw a couple of people still standing. That was the thing about a gunfight; nobody had more than six opportunities to hit somebody with a bullet. Only revolvers had even that many shots. Most of them had one pistol and one rifle, so they had two shots. Those had been long expelled. The men had mostly pulled knives and were facing off with two remaining white men. The smoke was settling and the shape of the field was becoming clear. There were two white men standing and about a dozen Native Americans. Joe Lewis looked around, surveying the bodies on the ground. He nodded to himself then looked up at the two remaining white men.

Joe Lewis smirked, "It seems that the Lord has made his judgment."

One of the white men shouted, "You'll pay for this."

"For what? All things are possible through the Lord. If he had not ordained this righteous action, he would not have allowed us to perpetrate." He pointed at the different Native Americans standing around. "Look at this. Not a single Indian has been killed." He pointed at the men dying in the dirt. "Look at these white men. We are still alive and you are dying. Who is it the Lord favors?"

One of the white men, having heard enough, ran at Joe Lewis. Joe knelt down, picked up the Walker Colt from the dirt. He cocked the hammer, took a knee and shot the man in the forehead. He hit the ground without slowing down, dead before his chin hit the dirt. Joe Lewis pointed at the other white man whose hands shot up.

"Please," the man shouted. "Mercy."

Joe Lewis nodded, but didn't lower his gun. "Hmm. Mercy?" He took a deep breath. "Through this holy unction and His own most tender mercy may the Lord pardon thee whatever sins or faults thou hast committed by sight by hearing, smell, taste, touch, walking, carnal delectation. May the Passion of our Lord Jesus Christ, the intercession of the Blessed Virgin Mary, and of all the saints, whatever good you do and suffering you endure, heal your sins, help you to grow in holiness, and reward you with eternal life."

The gun barked and the man fell to the ground with a hole in his neck.

Joe Lewis cocked the pistol again and started walking towards the house. "Now, where's his wife?"

━━━━━━━━━━

The banging on the door shocked Narcissa out of her silence. She had been sitting in a corner of the hallway with her knees pulled up to her chest and her face in her knees. The thundering of gunshots overlapped like waves crashing against a shore or thunder rumbling as a storm rolled into town. Then they'd fallen silent. She thought that meant it was over. She waited for something to happen. Then she heard boots on the porch and her stomach dropped. Whoever was banging on the door was obviously the winner. She hoped it was her husband.

"Who is it?" She screamed.

"I am a man of the Lord and I'm here about the Lord's work."

Not her husband.

"Is Marcus dead?" She shouted at the door.

The man on the other side of the door replied, "Not yet. In fact, you might be able to save him." She didn't know if that was a lie.

"How do I know I can trust you?" She asked.

In a scarily casual voice, the voice said, "You don't have a choice really. Could you ever live with yourself if you let him die?"

She thought about it for a little while. Could she live with herself if Marcus died in the dirt because she'd been scared? She crawled to her feet and walked to the door the way someone walks to the gallows. She put her hand on the doorknob and wondered if that was going to be the last thing she ever did. Had she lived a life the way she wanted? Would she be okay if this was the end of her life?

They were different questions. She'd definitely lived her life the way she had wanted. She had been comfortable and spent her time trying to help people and do right by them. She had been a missionary about the business of spreading the gospel of Jesus Christ. The great commission from Jesus himself had said to go forth and minister to all nations. She had tried to bring that ministry to the Cayuse and she was about to get killed for it. But she thought she might be okay with that. She could look the Lord Jesus in the eye and say that she had given everything she had. But if she protected herself and let Marcus die in the melon patch, she would never be able to live with herself. It wasn't worth it to save herself and lose her soul in the process. And so she turned the doorknob and opened the door.

She saw an Iroquois man with a Walker Colt in his hand. She didn't hear the gunshot that killed her.

1850

A few years passed and the bodies of Marcus Whitman, Narcissa Whitman, and eleven other white people were dust that had been returned to the earth. But the state of Oregon did not forget the Whitmans. They had taken to calling the act of killing the Whitmans the Whitman Massacre. It had gone on even after they killed Narcissa. Joe Lewis took about fifty hostages and waged a personal war against the United States. The army had managed to negotiate the release of the hostages; just like that, Joe Lewis retreated from history and disappeared into mystery. Nobody who had been at the Whitmans' farm that night could say precisely what Joe Lewis looked like. Most of them agreed that he was half-Iroquois. Some of them said he was part Iroquois and part White. Others said he was part Negro. A few even remembered him speaking in a different language that wasn't English or Iroquois. It could have been his native language they said. They said they thought he was from the islands -- no one was quite sure which islands exactly. Others said he was speaking in tongues; they say that when the shooting started, he had been engulfed in leaping flames but not consumed, like the burning bush that Moses encountered. He'd killed all thirteen of the white people with fire that leapt from his hands.

Whatever the truth had been, it was lost by 1850. By that time, the fervor of the white Oregonians had turned into a full-on conflagration and the heads of some Indians needed to roll if they were going to be satiated. To that end, several Cayuse -- five, to be exact -- had turned themselves in as participants in the Whitman Massacre. Two of the five men were bent-backed Cayuse men who had to be at least 70 years old. They were tired and gray-haired. Could they have committed a massacre three years earlier? They could have, the Judge supposed. But it was unlikely.

The others were men in their sixties as well. The five men were a sad and fatigued lot of men paraded onto the gallows with their heads in black bags. The raging mass of white people chanting and jeering and shaking their fists probably knew that these five old men weren't the young gun-wielding Cayuse who had killed the Whitmans in their house. They had to know; it was painfully obvious. They didn't care, though. They wanted blood. Three years had passed since the end of the massacre, and the authorities hadn't found who had actually done it. It wasn't about making it right now; it was about getting revenge. If these old men had to be hanged to make them feel a little bit better, they were okay with it.

The sheriff slipped the nooses around the heads of the Cayuse men. He cinched the heavy braided rope tight over their necks. The sheriff took a step back, his boots thudding against the wooden gallows. It was truly astounding how quickly local carpenters had put together the gallows. It was as if they had been waiting for three years for the chance to put together a hanging station.

The sheriff took a step back and looked to the crowd of angry white people. He took a deep breath and let out a strained sigh. He looked at them one more time, pleading with his eyes that something absurd was happening. He looked from the crowd, back to the black-bagged men with the curved backs hanging their heads. His eyes slid back to the people in the crowd. They were unrelenting. They wanted the blood of these men; they wanted to see them jerking on the end of a rope. Their eyes were crazy and angry and wide while the sheriff's were just sad.

He took a grip of the wooden lever, his hand sweating into the wood. He looked one last time at the crowd. They were screaming and pumping their fists. They weren't necessarily the ones who unsettled the sheriff. The ones who really shook him to the core were the ones who were calm. They stood there calmly smoking cigarettes or puffing on pipes and watching the men waiting to die. Resolved to this injustice, he took a deep breath and yanked the wooden lever. The lever, connected to a wooden rod, pulled the pins out of the trapdoors underneath each man's feet. The door under each man's feet flopped open, and the men dropped. They dropped a foot or two and jerked to a stop as the noose drew tight and the rope pulled taut. The men, each one past the prime of his life, jerked and twitched at the end of the rope.

You could set a noose to snap a man's neck if you wanted it to be quick. That was the kind of noose you tied when you were after justice. But when you were after revenge, you tied a different kind of noose. You tied a noose and didn't make the drop too long. That way, when the trapdoor opened, the man wouldn't fall far enough to snap his neck. Instead, he'd choke to death as the rope strangled him for what felt like an hour. His eyes would bulge out of his head, his mouth would fall open and finally, when his soul left his body, he'd void his bowels. It was a shameful, excruciating way to die.

That's the way these men died. They died with the blood vessels in their eyes bursting, their lungs collapsing, and feces running down their legs. To the red-faced white people in the crowd, it was the only just end to these men even though everyone knew they had nothing to do with the death of Marcus and Narcissa Whitman. Joe Lewis had faded into the realm of myth, so these men had to take the fall for his mob justice.

Jerking at the end of a rope, they might just be saving the Cayuse tribe from the metastasizing wrath of white men with guns. That's why these old men had chosen to be martyrs for the cause; they wanted to save their tribe from grave danger and no danger was greater or more grave than angry white men with guns.

VI

Blackie had never killed anyone before; he'd never had much reason to. He mostly kept his head down, delivered his ice, and went home. He liked mint tea and fishing to calm him down after a long day. He was a man of simple pleasures, short sentences, and plain language. It was the kind of thing many people demanded a Native be. In towns like Walla Walla, a man like Blackie was treated as a second-class citizen because he was a Native. His father used to tell him that there were two kinds of Natives: fighters and survivors. He never said that one was better than the other, but that a Native had to choose which kind he was going to be. A fighter, his father said, was someone who couldn't stand being treated like dirt by white men simply for being Native.

A fighter would fight back against the endless kinds of oppression that white men visited on Natives. A fighter would shout back, refuse to answer to "injun", throw his fists, and look a white man in the eye. If a sign in front of a business said a Native couldn't go in, a fighter would loudly walk right through the front door and dare anyone to stop him. That's what a fighter did. A survivor kept his head down and took it. If a business said no "injuns," a survivor would go to a different business. Or a survivor would find a white person to go and buy whatever he needed on his behalf. You had to be a lot smarter and lot more patient to be a survivor. Throwing your fists and raising your voice didn't take much intelligence or patience.

Fighters tended to look down on survivors; at least, they did when Blackie was young. There weren't many still alive now. In fact, there weren't any Cayuse left. Too many fighters, Blackie reckoned.

There was a common misconception, though. Blackie's father had the same misconception. He said that you had to choose between being a fighter and a survivor. He talked about them as two completely distinct ideas. But, he miscalculated one thing; he didn't account for people who had to fight to survive.

Blackie had always been a survivor. Natives were frowned upon in Walla Walla, so Blackie got a job that would make him indispensable. Selling ice, he was welcomed everywhere in town when no other Native would be. He wasn't allowed to own property in Walla Walla, so he got a cabin way out in the mountains where no one would find him. If they didn't want him around then he wouldn't be around. It worked out well, though. It fit his nature. He was naturally quiet and humble. He knew his own worth and no amount of name-calling and bigotry could change his own self-worth. He was a natural-born survivor. But now, he had to fight to survive.

That's what brought him to the moment he was at. He had a satchel bouncing around on his hip full of ammunition and the rifle strapped across his back. It was the rifle from the tavern -- the one with the etching of the Lewis and Clark expedition on it. Natives weren't allowed to buy ammunition in Walla Walla, so Debbie had bought it for him. She'd given him a stern talk that bordered on loving and maternal. She had been happy that he was taking a rifle with him, but was obviously quite frightened that something horrible would happen to Blackie.

The sun hadn't come up yet, but the sky was starting to turn light gray. That was a sign that sunrise would be soon and he'd be late for his day of delivering ice. So, he had to hurry.

Blackie jogged down the trail leading from his cabin to Walla Walla. He normally took the first fifteen minutes of his day to stretch his muscles. He couldn't afford to pull or strain a muscle while delivering ice; it was his only livelihood and the city would swelter and wilt without ice. Today, he'd skipped his morning stretching routine. He'd taken that extra fifteen minutes or so to jog lightly down the trail. About a half-mile down the trail, he found a massive cedar tree thick with leaves. He climbed up the tree until he thought he would be invisible from the ground.

He fished around in his satchel until he found one round. By 1904, metal cartridges had become the standard. Pretty much every gun carried by anyone in Walla Walla shot metal cartridges. However, there were a few people who were enthusiastic about the firearms of the Civil War and the American Revolution, so one general store in Walla Walla kept a supply of paper cartridges in stock. The rifle Blackie carried from the tavern was an early 18th century rifle, at least a hundred years old.

Blackie set the paper cartridge in the crook of a branch where it would be stable. He could only hope that it didn't rain. The paper cartridge was a sheet of paper rolled like a cigarette. It had a charge of 90 grains of black powder and a .50 caliber lead ball. The whole thing was sealed with pig fat. It could survive a little bit of humidity and moisture, but it wouldn't' hold up to any actual rain. He would have to hope.

With the paper cartridge placed properly, Blackie

climbed down from the tree and kept running. He found another tree a little bit off the trail. It was almost invisible from the trail, but if he got high enough, he could look down on the trail for about a mile in each direction. He set two paper cartridges in the crook of a branch there.

He put a few more cartridges in trees along the way. Finally, as he closed in on the mouth of the trail, where it opened up to Walla Walla, he climbed up a tree and stashed the rifle. It was charged, primed, and loaded. He didn't have much practice shooting a flintlock rifle. He knew how it was done, and he knew the basics, but he didn't know if he'd be any good at it. Luckily, Blackie was a very calm person. He just needed to stay calm and everything would be alright. The rifle had a separate, finer grain black powder for priming the pan. He stashed that with the rifle too.

Finally, he put his satchel in the tree. He hopped down from the tree and jogged into town just like any other day. He'd never killed anyone before, but as he hoisted the block of ice onto his back and groaned under its weight, he thought that by the end of the day, he would be a different person.

———

Owen and Frobisher were busy that day. They couldn't catch Blackie on their own. They'd come to terms with that truth. The ice carrier was just too fast. All those years of toting ice around on his back, running from saloon to restaurant to hotel had made him something they just couldn't contend with. That brought them out to the Burning Bush Ranch outside Walla Walla. They knocked on the door of the ranch house, still reeking of whiskey.

The rancher, John Langley had spotted them coming

from about a mile out and been waiting on them. He swung the heavy oak door of the ranch house open almost as soon as they knocked. Langley was a thin, sharp-eyed man with an angry stare and long jowls. His cheeks sagged almost as far down as his mustache which dripped down past his chin and flapped in the breeze. It was gray as stormy clouds and matched the gloomy wisps of hair on his bald head. His head was spotted with angry, red sunburn that matched the tip of his nose. Further proof that a man as white-skinned as John Langley had no business in the arid West. He was there nonetheless and he owned everything as far as his eye could see and beyond.

Langley scowled at the two men. "The hell you two doing darkening my doorstep?"

Frobisher straightened up and put on his haughty nature. "My name is Frobisher. Yes, *that* Frobisher. This is my, um, associate Owen." Frobisher waited for some kind of acknowledgement that never came. Langley just lifted his eyebrows and waited. "Okay then," Frobisher went on, "we have a business proposal for you."

Langley grunted, "What business you boys in? I reckon I want no part of it."

"We're in the gold business, sir."

"Lots of gold," Owen added.

Frobisher agreed, "Indeed. A lot of gold."

Langley put his hand on the door as if he were about to close it. "Lots of folks around these parts in the business of gold. Not a one of them in the business of actually finding none." He closed the door but Frobisher stopped it with his foot.

The Butcher had anticipated this. Frobisher reached into his pocket and produced the nugget of gold from Blackie.

"How's this?"

Langley's eyes widened. He picked up the gold, hefted it a few times, and then tested it with his teeth. Satisfied that it was real gold, he said, "Where'd you get this?"

"That's why we're here," Frobisher said. "We need a little help, in, procuring the rest."

Langley replied skeptically, "Procuring? Sounds a lot to me like you're trying to say 'stealing'."

Frobisher rolled his eyes. What was it with all of these people who clutched their pearls at the thought of taking a little bit of gold from somebody else? Langley owned a sprawling ranch that stretched over a thousand acres. From what Frobisher could tell based on the massive ranch house and the ranch hands coming and going on healthy workhorses, he was doing pretty well for himself. He wasn't pulling gold out of the ground. He was pulling hay, wheat, and strawberries out of the ground. Not to mention all of the cows, sheep, and pigs roaming around all over his ranch. The ground was spewing wealth and John Langley was lapping it up. The Indians who had been here before would probably like their land back, but there was too much wealth in it for Langley. So, he was okay with stealing land and wealth from Indians, but only in a roundabout way. That's the way so many people out here were though. You couldn't take a man's purse or his wife, but you could take his land. You could promise to pay him and then shortchange him; there wasn't nothing wrong with any of that. But taking wealth directly? Oh, that was the only taboo. It was foolishness, and this man needed to see that.

Frobisher shook his head, "No, sir. I ain't intending to take nothing but what you've already taken."

Langley cocked an eyebrow. "Me?"

Frobisher flailed his hand around at the massive ranch. "This ranch here used to be Indian land, I assume."

"It did," Langley said.

"You pay rent on the use of their land?" Frobisher asked.

Langley rolled his eyes, "Everything we do here is above board. We have contracts…"

Frobisher chuckled. "Everybody knows them contracts was drawn up to squeeze the injuns. You know it, I know it. Hell, the damn cows even know it. I ain't worried about that, though. What I'm about is just taking a little bit more out of the land the same way you fetch them strawberries off their plant."

Langley crossed his arms defensively. "I'm listening."

"Well, I know a place where there's a creek that's just lousy with gold nuggets. Bigger than that one you got in your hand." Frobisher decided to try and upsell it. "I seen it too. I seen nuggets big as a man's fist."

Langley asked skeptically, "Then why are you here and not there?"

Frobisher nodded. "That's what I'm getting to, sir. There's an Indian, a real fast Indian. He's trying to keep the gold all to himself."

"So, we are talking about stealing," Langley said.

Frobisher shrugged. "Only from an Indian."

Langley thought about it. He clucked his tongue. He unfolded his arm and adjusted his belt, a decidedly more open posture. "Okay, what do you need from me?"

Frobisher said, "A few horses and a few good men with hard hearts and big guns."

"I want forty percent of the yield," Langley said.

Frobisher whistled at the size of the figure. "Wooweee, I can't do forty. I can do fifteen."

Langley re-folded his arms. "Twenty-five. Final offer." He extended his hand. "We got a deal?"

Nightfall saw Blackie Sullivan strolling towards the edge of town. He had his hands in his pockets and was whistling quietly. He was trying to project the image of calm but really, his heart was racing. He'd spent all day doing his job the way he always had, but there was a knot in his stomach. His heart would peak and race every time somebody stepped out of a saloon or walked up behind him. He was jumpy as a stray cat all day long.

The day had ended and he'd packed up to go home. Nearing the edge of town, he knew the men would be after him soon. The first time they'd tried to follow him, he'd been legitimately unconcerned. He'd never met a single person who could keep up with him on foot, especially not a white person. The white people who lived in Walla Walla spent too much of their time on ranches, drinking in saloons, and sitting around their houses. He spent all day five days a week running ice back and forth. In fact, he thought he probably ran more than the professional runners. Not too long ago, an international competition had been set up in Greece. This year, it was coming to Missouri. The Olympics, they called it. It was supposed to mimic the old games from Ancient Rome. Blackie had read an article recently about how much the athletes were training.

Blackie didn't know how many miles he ran per day or how quickly he ran, but it really felt like a lot more than these athletes were supposedly training. One of them could maybe catch him on foot but these men from Walla Walla weren't going to catch him. Now, though, they had a new plan. Now they were ready to kill to get his gold. He wasn't a man who wanted to kill anybody, but he was going to do it to survive. If he had to be a fighter or a survivor, he was going to be a survivor. Today, that meant surviving by fighting.

He reached the edge of town and started towards his home. That's when he heard the first hoof beats. He couldn't tell exactly how many horses were behind him but it was more than two or three. The overlapping patter patter of hooves sounded like at least five and they were coming fast. The last time these men had pursued him, there had only been two of them. They'd been on foot, and they tried to follow. Judging by the sound of the hooves coming fast, they were not trying to follow him. They were going to run him down and kill him. He had to run, and he had to run fast.

The Indian must have heard the rush of horses because he took off running. It was the damndest thing to see, too. One second, he was walking casually towards the woods, then the next second, he was at a full sprint. His legs un-coiled and powered forward like a deer's legs. He bounded into the woods, barely kicking up any dirt. Honestly, it looked like his feet weren't even touching the ground. Those bare feet just kind of hovered over the edge of the ground. He disappeared into the woods.

Owen cursed. "Dammit."

Frobisher gigged his horse to a faster gallop and flew onto the narrow trail after the Indian. Langley had sent three men along with them. Frobisher didn't remember their names and he didn't much care. They were silent men who didn't talk much.

One of them was a Negro who said his family had been working for Langley's family since they had a plantation in South Carolina. They started out as slaves, no doubt.

Probably weren't being paid much better than that now, but he was here nonetheless. The other two were white men who looked like they could be related. They'd grown up on Langley's farm, playing with Langley's kids when they were kids themselves. Langley had sent his most loyal men. The kind he could trust to get the job done and keep their mouths shut. There wasn't a lot anyone would say about a man accused of stealing gold from an Indian. Frobisher couldn't think really of who would care beyond some of the Indians, but if Langley could avoid even the accusation, that would be preferable. So, he sent along some loyal men who wouldn't speak of it ever again. In fact, the Negro was so quiet that Frobisher wondered if he could even talk. He could ride a horse though.

His horse was close up on the withers of Frobisher's horse. He was up in the stirrups, curled over the back of the horse like a jockey.

The crack of the gun is loud and close. So loud that Frobisher hears it ringing in his ear. Completely unconcerned with being stealthy now, Frobisher yelled, "Hold your damn fire. We can't even see him yet."

Owen, from behind him, yelled, "That wasn't us."

Frobisher took a chance to glance backward. He saw one of the white men Langley had sent with them slumped over in the saddle. The man's head lolled to one side of the horse and he just jostled with the motion of the horse. Taking a longer look, Frobisher realized the top of the man's head was missing. The horse was just going along with the other horses.

Frobisher shouted, "Jesus Christ. He's shooting at us."

Owen shouted back, "Where is he?"

The Negro pointed off to the side and said, "Shot came from that direction."

So, he can speak, Frobisher thought.

Frobisher pointed in that direction, "We'll, go check it out." He wasn't about to go himself but he didn't care if some Negro got his head blown off.

One less Negro in the world wouldn't be so bad, Frobisher thought.

The black man gigged his horse and went tramping off into the deeper woods. Frobisher kicked his horse and kept up in the direction of the trail.

———

Blackie was frozen in the tree for a minute. He'd never killed before, but there he was. He had pulled a trigger, a gentle twitch of his finger, and the top of a man's head had disappeared. Just because he wanted it, a man had been killed. A man with a family, a wife, some kids. A future. What had he stolen from the world by killing that man? Had he taken away the father of the man who cures small-pox? Had he robbed the world of the man who becomes the next U.S. senator from Washington? There was no way of knowing, but Blackie felt a profound hollow in his chest. He imagined it was where his heart had been. He told himself multiple times that he was just surviving. The only thing he'd taken from the world was a man who was willing to murder to gain a little bit of wealth for himself.

That might be true, but Blackie had changed. By moving his finger just a few inches, he had changed fundamentally who he was. A man could do and undo certain things. He could put on a job title and take off a title. Killing wasn't like that. Once you killed one person, you were a killer. There was no way to undo that. Even if he never killed again, he was always going to be a killer. History would remember him as a killer, as much as history cared to remember any Native, that is.

He resolved he'd have to deal with that later. Right now, he needed to figure out how to get to his next position. The men on the horses had thundered farther up the trail but one man was stomping through the woods on his horse, nearing Blackie's position. Holding his breath and scampering like a housecat, Blackie slipped out of the tree and dropped to the ground silently. He hit the ground quiet as a cat and jogged through the woods.

He ran the way he was taught to move through the woods. He'd learned to navigate the woods chasing his dad and his uncles. They weren't really his uncles, he didn't think. They were just men about his dad's age whom his dad called brothers. They taught him to him how to run through the woods. Most people were tempted to tiptoe, but that placed too much weight right on the balls of your feet or your toes. So, when you stepped on anything, your entire weight came down on that object and made a loud noise. No, you had to roll from the balls of your feet to the side and bend your knees. That dispersed your weight across the ground and made for softer landings. There was no way to run completely silently, but the wind rustling through the trees made for some cover if you were quiet enough.

The sound of the man on the horse tromping through the woods provided all the cover Blackie needed. He was almost completely silent. Blackie got back to the trail and broke into a full run. It wasn't a sprint. It was the kind of long-legged springy run that he used to get from place to place with ice on his back. He couldn't pump his arms fully while holding the rifle, but the weight wasn't a bother. It was practically weightless compared to the blocks of ice. Up ahead, he could hear the men on horses. He sprinted as close as he dared before he could see them. They were sitting on their horses, swinging their guns back and forth looking for him. The man in the lead had a gun Blackie had never seen before. It looked like the kind of gun out of a dime store novel. There wasn't even a cylinder. Where did the bullets go?

Blackie knew where his bullets were. They were in a tree almost directly above the heads of the men on horses. There were three of them now. The man on the horse who had been sent to look for him was somewhere behind him. Blackie had to keep pressing forward though.

He dropped to his belly in the dirt beside the trail. Like a cat, he crawled on his hands and toes through the woods. Picking where he put his hands and knees carefully, he was able to move quietly. He crawled through the woods until he was close enough to reach out and slap one of the men's horses. That's exactly what he did. He got to his knees and slapped the rump of the horse.

Shocked by the sudden jolt, the horse leapt forward, whinnying and bucking. It reared back and threw its rider to the ground. The other two horses, spooked by the startled horse took off at a full gallop up the trail. They quickly disappeared into the woods trying to wrangle their unruly horses. That left just the one man who had been dumped onto his back in the dirt. He rolled over onto his side, where he found himself face to face with Blackie Sullivan.

They locked eyes for a minute, both of them lying in the dirt. There was a quiet moment that seemed to stretch for hours. Neither one of them seemed to know what to do next. Blackie looked in this man's eyes and tried to convince himself that the man was evil, that he needed to die. All of that became irrelevant when the man took a deep breath in preparation for yelling.

Blackie lunged, landing on top of the man. He put his hands around the man's neck and squeezed. He could hear the man wheezing, trying to intake air. He squeezed harder. The man under him flailed with his arms, scratching at Blackie's face. One of his fingernails dragged a ragged tear through Blackie's forehead. The Cayuse pressed his knee against the man's arm and pinned him to the ground with his weight. He squeezed and squeezed.

Slowly, the man underneath him started to fight a little bit less. He struggled and wheezed a little less. Blackie felt like he'd been choking the man forever. His arms and hands were burning. His fingers were screaming for relaxation, but Blackie didn't let up. Finally, the man's eyes rolled back in his head, and he went lifeless.

Blackie rolled off the dead man and flopped onto his back. He gasped for air as if he had just been running. His shoulders were on fire. His arms and wrists ached. He took a deep breath and crawled to his feet. As he walked away from the man, he took one last look back at the man's dead body. When he'd shot the man with the rifle, he'd felt completely hollow but that wasn't the case. When he killed with his bare hands, strangling the life out of the man, that was true hollowness. He felt empty. He would have to reckon with that fact some time in the future. But, for now, he needed to keep pressing forward. He could deal with the emptiness in his core once his life was safe.

He broke into a jog until he found the next tree. With the agility of a leopard, he scampered into the tree and grabbed the next paper cartridge. He tore the end off with his teeth and dumped the black powder into the barrel. He rammed the ball into the barrel with the ramrod and set it back. It only took him a few seconds. He cocked back the frizzen and loaded the pan with the finer grain black powder. The rifle was ready to shoot. Considering he'd only practiced it once before trying it, he thought he did it pretty well. It only took him about a minute. He'd heard somewhere that Civil War soldiers could do it three times a minute.

He scampered up the tree a little higher. He looked down the trail, lit by the silvery glow of the heavy, bright moon. It was almost like daylight but in an otherworldly feel. Strangely enough, the metallic pallor of the light didn't look like the brightest part. His father had taught him how to see at night when he was still young. It was a set of skills you had to practice. The eyes weren't to be trusted the same at night as they were during the day. Instead of trying to look as hard as you can, squinting and staring hard, you had to relax to see at night. Your peripheral vision was much better at dealing with black and white and other darker subjects. So, to see at night, you needed to relax your eyes and try not to focus too hard. That meant you had to sit very still and watch for things that didn't actually fit.

Nature did a lot of things; it came in just about every possible form. However, it didn't come in straight lines. It did complex patterns, but not the big simple ones. So, Blackie moved up into the high perch in the tree and relaxed his eyes. He was looking for the two remaining men on horseback and the one man behind him. He relaxed his eyes and saw two hulking figures moving with a slow purpose up the trail. They were barely more than dark blurs. That was enough for Blackie, though. He put the rifle to his shoulder and pressed his cheek against the stock. He closed one eye and lined the sightpost up between the notched V on the back of the rifle. He took a long inhale and settled the front post of the sight on the dark blur in front. He let out a slow breath so that his hands would be steady and squeezed the trigger with an easy pressure. The trigger seemed to pull forever. Just when he was starting to relax the hammer dropped. The steel hammer dragged against the flint frizzen, spraying an arc of sparks into the pan. The pan flashed with smoke and there was a pause that seemed to hang forever. It was long enough to make Blackie think he'd loaded the gun improperly.

Then it barked. The rifle bellowed a minie ball and a jet of smoke into the night sky. The smoke filled the area around Blackie, and if anyone had the wherewithal to look for him, they could find him by the cloud of black powder smoke reflecting moonlight against the night sky. So, he scampered out of the tree with his rifle in hand, not even looking to see if the man had been hit. Either he had or he hadn't. Either way, Blackie had to move to his next position. He only had the one bullet stashed in that spot.

He'd stashed the bullets in different places instead of carrying them around because he needed to be able to keep at least one hand free when he was running around. If he was trying to fiddle with a satchel, it would just waste even more of his time that he needed to be moving to his next perch. So, he headed for his next sniper nest.

The rifle barked somewhere behind them. It sounded far off with the dull wallop of a muzzleloader. Frobisher's gun hollered with a loud crack. This was something different. It sounded like a hollow thud that was infinitely more threatening than any modern gun that had ever been invented.

Owen's hands snapped to his chest. He groaned. He looked down at his hands; blood was seeping through his fingers, gushing with each racing heartbeat. His mouth fell open. He looked up at Frobisher and pleaded with the man with his eyes as if begging him to do something.

Frobisher didn't know what to say. He'd seen a wound like that once. He'd seen a man's chest geysering blood down the front of his shirt. He knew what came next. From the look in Owen's eyes, he knew what was coming next too.

Owen flapped his mouth as if he was going to say something but instead his eyes rolled back in his head. He tipped forward and thudded in the dirt. The blood rushing from his chest actually sped up for a minute. He gushed so much blood that the earth couldn't drink it fast enough. The blood started puddling around him until there was a muddy syrup underneath his horse's feet. Then, just that quickly, it sputtered and stopped. Owen was empty of blood. He was dead. Frobisher lifted his head and spun his horse in a tight circle, flailing his fancy new pistol in every direction. He couldn't' see anything though. He strained and strained, squinting harder and trying his best to focus in on the woods around him. He couldn't see a damn thing.

His heartbeat was starting to race which made it even harder for him to hear. He knew he needed to be quiet to hear the Indian scampering through the woods, but all he could really hear was the whickering of his horse and the sound of his own heartbeat. The more anxious he got, the faster the blood pumped into his ears. Eventually, he just heard blood thundering. The hammering in his ears was just as quickly as the blood that had spurted out of Owen's chest.

"To hell with it," Frobisher spat.

He turned his horse uphill and gigged it with his heels. The horse lurched into action and sprinted towards the top of the hill.

The black man emerged from the woods again. He came stomping out of the woods somewhere ahead of where he'd gone into the woods. He was leading his horse by the reins now and walking in front of it. That was a good choice, Blackie thought. If you knew how to move through the woods, it could be much easier to move through by leading your horse. Horses weren't necessarily the loudest walkers but they definitely didn't care anything about stealth. They were faster than just about any prey that might try to feed on them, so they usually just relied on running as fast as possible. That's why they didn't like moving through the woods. Confined spaces made it harder for them to move around. They liked wide open spaces. If you wanted to move your horse quietly through the woods, the best way to accomplish that was to lead it on foot. So, the black man came leading the horse on foot.

Blackie thought he was probably the most intelligent of all the men who were pursuing him. The man was a little bit ahead of him, scanning the area as he walked. Then, he locked eyes with Blackie. Blackie was already in a full sprint. He pumped his arms and legs like pistons, eating up ground with each stride. Eventually, he was only a few strides away from the man. The man dropped the reins and fumbled in his waistband for his gun. Or probably a knife. Blackie didn't know. He just knew he had to get there before this man produced whatever weapon he was looking for.

Still in stride, Blackie tossed the rifle up in the air, flipping it slowly. He caught it again with his hands on the barrel. He planted his lead foot, swung his hips, and used his sprint momentum to bring his hands around. He swung the rifle by the barrel like a baseball bat. Still moving as fast as he could, the stock of the rifle caught the man in the mouth. His head jerked to the side. His jaw crunched like a foot stepping on dry leaves. Teeth skittered out of the man's mouth, glittering in the night sky before they sprinkled to the ground. He spun on his heels and dropped into the dirt. As he fell, a knife skittered out of his pocket.

A knife then.

Blackie knelt down and picked up the knife. It was a massive Bowie knife -- the kind that was made popular at the Alamo in Texas when those men fought so hard to keep their slaves. He picked up the slaveowner knife and studied the enormous blade. Without a second thought, Blackie drove the slaveowner knife between the man's shoulder blades. He squirmed for a second then fell still. Blackie left the knife in his back.

One man left. Blackie hopped on the back of the black man's horse and gigged it into a gallop.

Frobisher was now in a full gallop up the mountain. He wasn't going to die out here in the dirt like a dog, and he definitely wasn't going to let some Indian keep him from getting his gold. Who was this man? Frobisher had thought Blackie was just the longhaired Indian who carried ice around town. Four people had died though and he hadn't even seen Blackie. That's when Frobisher figured it out: he was running into a trap.

He wasn't running from Blackie; he was running into his death. There wasn't just one person; that couldn't be possible. Blackie Sullivan had to be three or four people. At least, the ones killing them in the woods that night had to be multiple people. They'd been killed almost a mile apart on this damn trail. There was no way one person could get a mile up a wooded trail faster than horses. He'd been set up. Who could have set him up? He thought it might have been the butcher. Could the butcher have set up some kind of side deal with the Indian? No way. The butcher would never work a redskin. It had to be Blackie's doing. He had known they were going to follow him and had recruited some of his Indian friends to lie in wait for them.

Damn, he thought. Those Indians were so deceitful. Hiding in the woods so they could pick them off like fish in a barrel. His hatred for Indians tripled in that moment. Maybe even quadrupled. Once for every Indian hiding in the woods and shooting them. If the black man was still alive, there were only two of them. But it was more likely that the Indians had already killed him. Now, Frobisher was all alone.

He spotted a clearing up ahead and figured that must be Blackie's house.

"I made it," he laughed. "Holy sh…"

———————————

The man looked like he was laughing when Blackie pulled the trigger. Had he known that Blackie had caught up to him? Had he seen his death and found something funny in the afterlife? Was he in the Happy Hunting Grounds now? Surely not. Not someone so deceitful. The top of his head slid off in a way Blackie had never seen before. It was as if the bullet had been a saw instead of a ball of lead.

The top of the man's head seemed to leap off the rest of his body as if it were just cleanly detached. Blood burst from the back of his head like the smoke bursting out of the barrel of the rifle. He slumped before falling to the ground like a sack of potatoes and thudding lifeless in the dirt. His head leaked blood into the dirt making a crimson-brown slurry thick as gravy.

Blackie sat on the back of the horse for a minute. He rested the rifle across his lap and slumped over the saddle. He rested his head on the saddlehorn and took a deep breath. That was the last of the men. He'd been promising himself that he would wait until they were all dead to allow himself to feel what he'd done. Now, alone in the woods with five dead bodies, he found himself searching for anything that he thought he should feel -- sadness, regret, sickness. There was none of that. He felt something that he had been feeling ever since he pulled the trigger on that first man and that had multiplied when he'd strangled the next one. He felt hollow. There was nothing in him that would feel bad for them. He thought he would be sick with himself for what he'd done, but something about him just couldn't feel it.

He thought that it was the memory of the Cayuse in his blood. He didn't really subscribe to the idea that one Cayuse could carry the memories of all the other Cayuse in his genetics, but there was something there. He had never been alive when the Cayuse were proud and plentiful in the Northwest. By the time he'd been born, there were only a few remaining. His dad had been the last full-blooded Cayuse and he'd died a few years ago. Now Blackie was alone, but on some level he felt like he had done something that no Cayuse had been able to do. He had been able to stake a claim in the world of white men and hold back their advance. There were Cayuse who had fought against the white men, of course. And there had been others who chose to flee north into Canada.

How long would this last? Would more people discover his gold? Would more people want to kill him to take it? In fact, he wondered how they had even found out about his gold. He typically changed his gold for greenbacks at the bank in Walla Walla. He'd been taking gold to the bank for years, though. His father had taken the gold to that bank before him. It couldn't be that. It had to be something else. What had changed? Was there someone new working at the bank? Not that he knew of. It was possible somebody at the bank had mentioned in passing that he routinely brought gold to the bank.

The butcher. The bank had been closed last time he'd had to do any shopping so he'd paid in gold. The butcher had seen the gold. That had to be it. He had been betrayed by the butcher. He gritted his teeth. Would the butcher send more people after him when those didn't come back? Or would he give up entirely?

Blackie sat down and thought about how he'd been determined to be a survivor but had ended up as a fighter. What would a survivor do with the bodies? Should he leave a trail of dead bodies to scare the butcher away? No, the white people in this area already thought that Indians were half-magical. He would bury the bodies and never speak of it to anyone in public. The unknown would serve him much better than any kind of truth. If he could maintain an air as a mythical Indian, maybe the butcher would leave him alone.

He walked the horse up to the horse where the last man had died. His dad had taught him a thing or two about horses. This one was tall and lean. Its chest was deep and its muscles rippled under the fur. Its coat was brushed carefully and glimmered with the shine of one well-fed. If he had to guess, it was a thoroughbred and an expensive one at that.

For the first time since his frenzied chase after the last man, Blackie looked down at the horse he was on. It was a little shorter than the thoroughbred. It was a stout muscular thing that seemed to never want to sit still. Blackie thought it was one of the new kinds of horses that many people had taken to calling quarter horses.

An idea dawned on him. He leaned over and grabbed the reins of the thoroughbred. He walked the horses towards his house. He needed a shovel to bury the bodies first.

Blackie showed up to grab his first blocks of ice. The sun was just cresting over the treetops, and Blackie found himself exhausted. His feet dragged as he got into town and walked towards his work. He had spent so much time the night before running through the woods. He thought it was more than just a physical exhaustion though. It was the same hollowness that had plagued him all night. He'd turned into something that he couldn't turn back from. He would always be a killer. He hadn't killed just one or two either. It was five. Out here in the Northwest there weren't too many veterans of the Spanish-American War from a few years ago, but Blackie had encountered a few. They didn't seem particularly damaged by their time in war, but there was something that they all shared. They all seemed to yearn for solitude. They were drawn to the Northwest because of the endless expanse of nature and the limitless possibilities.

If you wanted, you could head out into the woods of Oregon or Washington and not see another soul for weeks. Blackie understood that now. Once you had shot someone and once you had strangled the life out of someone, you looked at human beings differently. Walking towards his work, Blackie couldn't help but look at the rise and fall of the chests of the people he passed. He looked at their necks and couldn't help but imagine his hands slipping around their throats. He didn't want to kill them by any means, but he knew for a fact that he could do it. The very idea that he knew he could kill them made him want to keep his distance. It's like he didn't trust his hands anymore. By himself out in the woods, there was no one to make him doubt his own good nature. He already wanted to head back up the mountain and be by himself. He needed to keep the appearance of normalcy though.

The butcher needed to see him go about his day without any real care in the world. That would make the butcher think that he had somehow made his goons just disappear. The story would be just as important as the reality. He needed to be a myth.

He walked past Debbie's office. As soon as he shuffled past the open door, she bounded into the hallway after him. She grabbed his arm and pulled him into the office. He allowed himself to be pulled into the room.

She closed the door behind him and sat down on her desk. She folded her arms and waited. For a long while they just looked at each other.

She eventually said, "Well?"

"Well what?"

"Blackie Sullivan, you know what. What happened? With those men?"

"They won't bother me anymore," was all he said.

She grabbed his hand and squeezed it, maybe a little harder than she intended. "Where'd they go?"

Blackie just shrugged. He felt like he was looking right through her. "I don't know. Wherever bad men go when they die."

Debbie shrieked and covered her mouth her hands. Her eyebrows were up near her hairline. "You killed them?"

Blackie nodded. "I had to."

Debbie grabbed his hand again and pulled him down into a chair. Something about finally sitting down drained him all of his energy. He sank into the chair and felt it fold around him. He felt so small and yet so distant. It's like he was looking down at himself from afar.

Debbie sat on the desk and held his hand. "Tell me everything."

And he did. He told her about killing the men. He hunted them, he said. Hunted them like they were deer and killed them like a hunter. The only real difference was that deer are difficult to track and quick on their feet. These men were slow and loud. They followed a trail, and they seemed completely blind in the night. They were completely unprepared for being in the woods after dark. It wasn't even really hunting. When you were hunting, there was a chance your prey would get away. These men never stood a chance. They were slaughtered. That's what it was. It was a slaughterhouse.

"In a slaughterhouse," Blackie said, "some ranchers build these high walls and these curves. So, the cows can't see to either side of them and they can't see in front of themselves either. They can just see the walls on either side and the wall ahead. The rancher or a ranch hand, I guess, leads them through the curving tunnel. Eventually, they turn a corner and there's a man standing on a platform over their heads. And he's got a great big sledgehammer. That's what it was like."

Debbie is completely silent as he tells her the story. There's no inflection in his voice -- just a monotone. That's because he doesn't really know what to emphasize. How is he *supposed* to feel? He doesn't know, so he just feels nothing.

He keeps talking. "The trail was like the curved path. They met their death out there. Five men."

Debbie squeezed his hand. "It was you or them."

Blackie nodded. "It was me or them."

Debbie slid off the desk and pulled his hand to her side. She placed his hand on her hip and leaned forward. He kept his hand there, sliding it around to the small of her back. She placed her hand on either side of his face.

"I'm glad it was you," she said. He didn't respond. She said, "You're not a bad man, Blackie Sullivan. You're a fine man."

She kissed him, softly at first, then with more emotion.

———————————

Blackie walked into the Look-See and saw Looking Glass standing behind the bar, cleaning glasses. Blackie felt like he was always cleaning glasses. Maybe it was just a thing he did to keep himself busy.

Blackie handed the rifle to Looking Glass who studied it. Looking Glass took the rifle and sniffed the barrel.

Looking Glass said, "Ammonia? You cleaned it."

Blackie turned to leave. He nodded. "Yes. It can get corroded if you use it too much."

VII

1908

Blackie walked the quarter horse to the starting gates of the race. The weather that day was hot and dry. The track would be a quarter-mile of dust. He tied a bandanna over his face to counteract the sure cloud of dust that the other horses would kick up. He wasn't too worried about it, though. His quarter-horse, Isuuxh'e, didn't seem affected by the hot, dry weather. Isuuxh'e and the other horses Blackie had claimed from the men he'd killed lived with him and Debbie outside of Walla Walla. They were used to the hot, dry weather and wouldn't be affected.

This was a quarter-mile race, just a straightaway. That's why he'd brought Isuuxh'e. The horse, a quarter horse, was bred for nothing more than quarter mile. While Blackie felt confident that his horse could hold his own over a longer race, he had other horses for that. Isuuxh'e had never lost a race and Blackie wouldn't put him in a race that he wasn't meant to run. He wasn't here for the money, though Debbie had bet a few hundred dollars on Blackie. They would take the money and put it in the bank probably. He was here for something more simple and more important than money. He was here to prove that the Cayuse still ran the Northwest.

The Cayuse hadn't always had horses. Before the Europeans had brought horses to the continent, the Natives had moved on foot. In fact, Blackie was just like the rest of his people in that way. He had spent the first part of his life moving on foot. Now, the white people had brought him a horse. The difference was in who died. Typically, it was the Cayuse who were buried in unmarked graves. This time, it had been the white people.

And here Blackie was again, to remind the white people who first conquered the wild, untamed Northwest. He was going to run this race and prove that they couldn't ever truly exterminate the Cayuse.

Blackie and Isuuxh'e walked up to the starting chutes for the race. Blackie patted the side of Isuuxh'e. "You ready to fly, little brother."

The horse shook its mane in response.

Blackie straightened up. He looked to his side and saw a couple of white men with sunburnt red noses sitting on horses. Their horses looked well-fed and well-cared for. They were thoroughbreds, though. They couldn't compete with his quarter horse. To his right, he saw three men sitting on horses. Only one of them was on a quarter-horse. He was a small man with a thin nose. He was smaller than Blackie and his horse looked well-muscled with a deep chest. That man was going to be a serious challenger.

Blackie could raise his horses as well as possible, and he did. He raised them the Cayuse way. But there was nothing he could do to be smaller. While a horse could comfortably carry about one-third of its weight, it still helped for the jockey to be as small as possible. Even ten or fifteen pounds could make the difference in a close race.

Blackie couldn't be smaller, though. He would have to just hope that Isuuxh'e was faster than this man's horse.

A man standing to the side of the race track stepped up and put his mouth to a cone shaped bullhorn. The judge hollered into the bullhorn, "Jockeys, on your marks. Get set." He lifted a revolver into the air. Blackie took a deep breath and let it out. He tightened his hands on the reins, his sweaty hands gripping the leather so tightly it creaked. He lifted his butt out of the saddle and braced himself in the stirrups.

He didn't need to do much; Isuuxh'e knew what to do. The gun went off with a bark, and the horses took off. It was quickly apparent where the race was going to be. After a few strides, Blackie and the other man on the quarter horse were in the front. Blackie looked over to his left but didn't see anybody. The men on the thoroughbreds had already been left behind. He looked to his right and only saw the thin man on the quarter horse. They actually locked eyes as the dust started to kick up.

Many people said that a quarter-mile race was just a sprint. It was definitely a sprint but that's not all it was. It took more planning than many people realized. Those who didn't plan properly had to rely on having the fastest horse from start to finish. Blackie's hope was that this man on the fine quarter horse had always been the fastest horse in the race and had never had to learn any technique. This wasn't the fastest Isuuxh'e could run. The horse was matching the thin man's horse stride for stride and just waiting for the signal from Blackie.

Some people tried to kick for the last stretch of the race and sprint out ahead of their competition. Blackie liked to slowly kill his competition. He squeezed Isuuxh'e in the ribs and the horse started to speed up. It didn't jump out ahead; it just sped up enough to start pulling away from the man on the other quarter horse. As long as Blackie squeezed Isuuxh'e, the horse would continue speeding up. Very gradually, they started to pull away from the man on the quarter horse. He looked up long enough to see that Blackie was pulling away. He whipped the horse with his wooden riding crop, slapping its flank with a loud popping sound. The horse sped up a little but it was obvious to Blackie that the man's horse didn't have anything left.

As Blackie and Isuuxh'e continued to spread the distance between them, the man started whipping harder and harder. The finish line was too close though. Blackie relaxed on squeezing his horse. The horse sprinted past the finish line a few seconds before the thin man. The thin man crossed a few seconds later. He threw down his riding crop and spat into the dirt.

"Worthless beast," he shouted and slapped the side of his horse.

Blackie walked his horse over to the man. The others on the thoroughbreds were just now starting to finish. Blackie leaned towards the man who was still slapping the back of his horse.

"Please don't do that," Blackie said.

"What did you say to me?" The man shouted.

Blackie straightened up in his saddle, "I said, please don't do that. It is not the horse's fault."

The man shouted back, "If it ain't his fault, injun, whose fault is it?"

Blackie turned Isuuxh'e and started walking away. He said, "Well, there's only you and the horse."

The man kept shouting and cussing him out behind his back, but Blackie didn't worry about it. The judge handed him an envelope heavy with dollar bills.

"Thank you," Blackie said. He and Isuuxh'e started to walk away.

The judge said, "You're not going to count it?"

Blackie shook his head. "I don't care."

Debbie came jogging up to him. She was wearing a long white sundress and a huge flopping hat that kept the sun off her. She was half-Native but she was still light enough that her skin would wither and burn under the endless sun in the summer. Without even worrying about her dress, she grabbed Blackie's arm and swung up into the saddle.

"Great job, honey," she said.

He smiled and said, "Thank you."

Debbie held out her hand over his shoulder and very dramatically cleared her throat. Blackie slapped the envelope of money into her hand.

"Thank you very much," she said.

They rode away from the racing track. There were a few more races that week and Blackie thought he'd stay around to see if he could win a few more races. Debbie liked to handle the money because she knew Blackie didn't care a bit, and he'd give all the money to the first hungry person who asked him.

━━━━━━━━━━━━━━

Always the one to worry about money, Debbie prodded and cajoled Blackie to put his money in a bank. The Cayuse man had been blessed with a fortune that was quite literally at his feet. The creek running next to his house, a slow-moving brook that tumbled over rocks and slowly wore them smooth over hundreds of years was peppered with nuggets of gold. The creek was only a stone's throw from the front porch of his and Debbie's house. If he wanted to spend a few hours one day fishing and relaxing, he could cast a line into a swirling pool in the creek and wait for the fish to bite. While he did that, he sometimes would dip a pan into the dirt at the bottom of the clear blue water and shake the pan until he rustled up a nugget of gold.

The way he understood it, that was pretty rare. Goldmining was sparking rushes to different parts of the country and driving people into the mountains of states that had never before seen so many people. These people -- prospectors they were called by the sympathetic -- hoped they could pull enough gold out of a river or a creek to strike it rich. Usually they were called dreamers or to some, just idiots. Most people who went out into the mountains to find their fortunes found nothing at all. Gold mining or gold prospecting was billed as something of a pretty safe bet by the Western companies when they were marketing to those in the snowy Northeast -- they offered a chance to come out to the warmer parts of the country and leave a rich man. The reality was that they didn't find much out there but heartache, poverty, and an impending death.

In fact, the prospects of hitting a vein of precious metal was so low that many people joked the only thing you could find out West was your tombstone. It was so common that the man who founded Tombstone, Arizona named his town for the saying. He'd found silver in Arizona, but most people had found only a hardscrabble life that ended in a painful death.

Not so with Blackie Sullivan. He'd lived at the house his entire life and the gold was just below the surface of the water. Sometimes, he went days and days without finding any but more often than not, he could pull up a nugget of gold after a few hours. He didn't do much searching for it -- didn't have much reason to.

He had rows of corn growing behind his house, a patch bursting with melons, and a few goats prowling around chomping on the grass. He had milk when he needed it, whichever vegetables he could coax out of the ground, and fresh water. In fact, the only thing he lacked was a steady source of meat, but buying meat had led to a life-changing event in the past. It was a chance encounter with a particularly vicious butcher that had led him to killing five men in the woods. But, like so much of Blackie's life, he had managed to even turn that into an opportunity for him. He took those horses, fine horses raised by men with wealth, and bred them until he had a stable of growing racehorses. Pretty much everyone who raised quality racehorses was outraged that Blackie would hitch his horses to a plow and pull them through the tough dirt to grow his crops, but he wasn't a soft man who came out to the West to find a fortune or build an empire. He was a Cayuse who was as much a part of the land as the horses on it and the vegetables coming from it.

His horses worked and they enjoyed all they could eat. If they wanted to run in races, they would. Blackie didn't force them into anything and he didn't treat them like they weren't incredibly powerful beasts. He had a stack of cash from winning races -- he assumed it was somewhere -- that said his way of raising horses was superior to the coddled sensibilities of his competitors.

That stack of cash -- wherever it might be -- and the gold he plucked out of the river were the reason he was in the bank in La Grande. He carried a satchel on his hip, heavy with refined gold and unrefined ore. He didn't like being in the bank and he didn't like having gold on him. The last time he'd shown his gold to a white man, he'd ended up killing five people in the woods. He didn't necessarily distrust all white men -- painting any group of people with such a broad brush would be a mistake. It was the kind of mistake people made over and over again about Natives. They thought the Apache were no different from the Shoshone and that they all were untrustworthy. He wouldn't sink to that kind of level, not even in his mind. But he was worried. He had seen how quickly one nugget of gold turned men into monsters. What could the amount he was carrying do? What would someone do to get his bag full of gold?

He hadn't weighed the gold he was carrying, but the way it was bouncing around on his leg said it was about fifty pounds. It was about the same weight as the blocks of ice he used to carry when he was running ice in Walla Walla. He had no problem with the weight, and he made an effort to carry it as if the satchel weren't heavy. He didn't want to signal to anyone that he might be carrying a lot of anything, especially not anything you would normally carry into a bank.

The doors were open to the bank and the fans were spinning overhead. Blackie didn't know much about the price of electricity but all of the spinning fans had to be incredibly expensive. His immediate thoughts were about the price of the electricity pumping into this bank and how many of his gold nuggets it would take to light his house. As the air circulating from the fan wicked the sweat off his forehead, he thought it might be a pretty good investment. Would that be just another thing a white man tried to steal from him, though? That was always in his mind, and it was definitely in his mind as he walked up to the counter of the bank.

The man sitting behind the counter was wearing a wool suit with his tie knotted up next to his throat. He looked absolutely miserable. Sweat ran down his forehead and the collar of his shirt was stained with salty sweat. He wiped his forehead with a handkerchief then put it back in his pocket. There was no amount of fanning that could save someone from the summer heat. He could take off the damn suit, Blackie thought.

The man behind the counter cleared his throat. His eyes narrowed as he studied Blackie. Blackie, dressed for the heat, was wearing linen pants and a shirt that opened around halfway down his chest. It was loose and breezy, perfect for the summer but horribly out of place in the polished wood bank. The man scrunched his nose and practically sneered at Blackie.

"Can I help you, son?"

Blackie nodded and said weakly, "I think so. I would like to, uh, make a deposit."

At that moment, he wished more than anything he had Debbie with him. He'd wanted to send Debbie to the bank with the gold. He thought that the bankers would be less likely to try to steal from someone they thought was white. Debbie could pass for white pretty easily, especially if she avoided the sun for a few days. But she'd pointed out that they might not steal from a white person, but they would steal from a lady. In fact, they probably wouldn't even allow a woman to open an account without her husband's written permission and he'd had to be present for that anyway. Whichever way they sliced it, Debbie and Blackie decided they were going to be taking a big risk.

"How much you looking to deposit, boy?"

"Blackie," he said. "My name is Blackie."

"Okay, boy, fine. My name is Hudson. It's fine to meet ya."

This was already off to a bad start. A Native man had to learn how to navigate an unkind world and that meant being aware of the warning signs. When you were picking your way through the woods, you had to keep an ear out for rattle of a snake's tail or the pitter-patter of wolf's paws. Those were warning signs out in the wild. In place like banks and courts of law, the predators were white men. They signaled their danger in different ways. One of them was calling anyone not a white man "boy." It was a way to remind someone, a grown man, that he didn't deserve the respect one gives to an adult. He was just a "boy." Blackie tried not to get too worried. Maybe this was just a way this man, Hudson, talked but he definitely took note of the warning.

"Is there a more private place we can, uh, discuss this transaction?"

Hudson rolled his eyes and wiped the sweat off his forehead again. "Boy, I don't have a lot of time. So, if you ain't got nothing to be serious about, why don't you just move it along?"

Blackie looked behind him and saw nobody in line. He looked around the bank and saw the only other person was a deputy sheriff sitting in a chair by the door with his feet up on a desk and his hat pulled down low over his eyes. The soft rise and fall of his chest indicated he was probably asleep.

Blackie reached into his satchel and grabbed the first nugget he could find. It was a fairly small one and unrefined. He set the rough rock down on the counter. The rock was dirty and gray but there were flecks of gold peeking out in different spots. Hudson's eyes got wide. He picked it up and inspected it. He dusted it off a little bit with his hand to inspect some of the gold.

"So, you got you some fool's gold. I'm proud of you."

Blackie responded, "It's not fool's gold. It's real."

He fished around in his satchel until he found one that he'd refined in his fireplace. It was smooth and round, the exact size of a musket ball. That was how Blackie refined all of his gold. He refined it in the same cast iron pot that his father had used to melt down lead to make musket balls. He'd poured the liquid gold into the musket ball mold and let it harden. Each one weighed only a few ounces. Blackie knew exactly how much each one weighed and so he knew exactly how much they were worth. That was how he would catch this man if he tried to steal from him.

Gold was selling for $21 an ounce according to the U.S. government. Each golden musket ball weighed one and a half ounces. If this man was being fair with Blackie, he would value each ball at $31.50.

Blackie set the golden musket ball on the desk and it rolled towards Hudson. He picked it up, tested the heft in his palm and then bit it with his molars. The musket ball came away with a scar from his teeth.

Hudson whistled, the air whining through his teeth.

"Where'd you get your hands on this, boy? You steal it?"

There's a silence as Hudson and Blackie stare at each other and the question hangs in the air. Blackie's mouth hangs open but he doesn't know how to respond. A smile crept across Hudson's face.

He started laughing; it's a big, deep laugh that shakes his whole body. "Oh, man, I'm just messing with you. You trying to deposit just these two?"

Blackie visibly relaxes. He lets out a sigh of relief and his shoulders lift as if he's no longer holding a weight. He realized at that moment that he'd been holding his breath and he's just now starting to breathe normally. He takes a breath and shakes his head. He's still a little worried that Hudson could be playing some kind of trick to get his money, but he has no choice but to trust this man. He's not going to trust him completely, but he can put a little bit of faith in Hudson's good nature. The banker has earned that much.

"No, actually, it's a little bit more." Blackie lifts up the satchel and places it on the counter with a heavy thud. The closing flap flops open and a few gold nuggets tumble out. Hudson's eyes nearly jumped out of his head. He was actually thrown back in his chair by the sight of the fifty pound sack of gold. The gold is rough ore that has to be cracked like a nut to get at the gold inside and smooth musket balls of solid gold.

Hudson whistles again and that morphs into laughter. "Whooweee. That's a lot of gold." He made the sign of the cross. "You have got to tell me where you got this. I got a wife and three kids and I'm tired of this job, I tell ya."

"I, uh, I'd rather not say. I had a bad experience once."

Hudson laughed and bounced a handful of gold in his hand. "I bet so. You better be glad the Lord came into my life a while back because I've thought about robbing you seven or eight times in the last 30 seconds. That ain't no lie." He started laughing again.

Blackie didn't know what to say but apparently Hudson was one of those men who didn't need a partner to hold a conversation. He went on talking.

"I met a gold prospector a few months back who had a gold nugget the size of his fist. It was the damndest thing I ever saw. I said to him, his name is Jed, you can ask him if you ever head to the bar down the road. I said to him, Jed, that's his name. I said Jed, I reckon I'll live from now until my dying day and never see this much gold in one place again. We both agreed. Boy were we wrong. Matter of fact, you should go down to the bar and tell Jed. Oh, actually, better not. Those gold prospectors are a bunch of roughnecks only out for a dollar. They'll rob ya just as soon as look at ya."

The door opened to the bank and a thin man with a short-sleeved button down shirt and a black tie slipped into the bank. Hudson shoved the gold back into the satchel and closed it up.

"That's Mormon Mickey. He prefers to be called Mickey. Works down at *The Observer*. Better not let him see your gold stash. He'll write about in the morning paper. By nightfall, somebody will be trying to rob you."

"Uhh, thanks."

Hudson smiled, "No problem, Blackie. Let's see about setting you up a bank account. Any idea how much gold you got in there?" He practically whispered the word "gold" while eyeing the newspaper writer.

In Hudson's office, little more than a crowded wooden box with a desk crammed into one corner, the temperature was unbearable. There was no electricity in the office, just a big window that let in the sunlight. The room was bright from the beaming sun outside but also hot like an oven. Another rash of sweat broke out across Blackie's forehead.

Hudson had to climb over the desk to get behind it. Blackie sat down in the chair. It was so close to the wall, he banged it pulling the chair out. Blackie curled himself up in the chair, and Hudson put the clanging bag of gold on the desk.

Hudson smiled, rolling one of the gold musket balls in his hand. "How much gold you reckon you got in here?"

Blackie shrugged. He wasn't ready to trust Hudson completely. "Well, each one of the balls is an ounce and a half. There's a hundred of them."

Hudson nodded. His eyes went distant for a second as he did the math in his head. "That's 150 ounces right there. Hmm, let me think. At $21 an ounce, that's... whooo. That's right at $3100. You got yourself a small fortune here, fellow."

Blackie cleared his throat, "I think it's $3150 actually."

Hudson's eyes glazed over again as he ran the numbers

in his head. "Well I'll be. You're right. You want that in a savings account or do you need a transaction account as well?"

Blackie scrunched his face. "Transaction account?"

Hudson nodded. "Mmhmm. Checking account, some people call it. We hold onto your money, in this case your gold, and you write a check that says you got money back here. Not everywhere accepts them. Too many drifters out here writing bad checks."

Blackie thought about it. It might be easier to buy things if he had a check and didn't just hand people a bunch of gold or cash. But what would people in town think of a Native with a checking account? Wouldn't that just lead them to believe he's hiding some kind of stash of money? Well, yes, Blackie thought. They'd *know* he's hiding a stash of money but it would be a stash at the bank. He decided against it. Better to keep his chips close to the chest.

"No, just the savings, sir."

Hudson rolled his eyes. "Why you calling me sir? Call me Hudson."

"Okay. Hudson."

"Well, Blackie, I think we are good to go." He started scribbling in a ledger book with his pen. Blackie saw his name, a date, $3150, and the designation "gold."

Hudson spun the ledger book around for Blackie to sign.

"We'll have to verify the gold balls with our smelting guy. They look good to me, but we'll see. I can set you up for the $3150 right now. Then we'll have to get the ore refined and so on. We can send you a report on how much it's worth in the post."

"The post? So, you need my address?"

Hudson nodded, "That's typically how that works."

Blackie shook his head. "No, I think I'll just come back in a few days and you can tell me in person."

Hudson lifted an eyebrow. "You're not in some kind of trouble are you?"

Blackie shook his head again. "No, and I'm trying to avoid getting into some kind."

Hudson sat back in his chair and laced his fingers across his stomach. He studied Blackie for a second. "Folks must not take kindly to an injun.. Pardon me, Indian, with all that money."

"They really don't."

Hudson nodded. "Okay, come back here in a few days and I'll get you up to speed."

Blackie stood up and shook Hudson's hand. Hudson stood up as well, clasping Blackie's hand in both of his.

Blackie turned to leave and stopped. He had to ask. He was running a pretty serious risk, but he needed to make it happen.

"Is it possible to deposit some more, when I come back?"

Hudson's eyebrows shot up to his hairline. "More? You got more?"

"Yes."

Hudson shrugged. "Sure thing. That's what a bank is for. How much you got?"

Blackie had weighed his gold in separate batches but he had a decent idea of how much.

Blackie practically whispered, "Five hundred pounds?"

The sheer size of it pushed Hudson back in his chair. He whistled and sat back in the chair. He opened his mouth to say something then closed it. "Wow. Um. Wow."

Hudson tapped his pen on the table for a minute while thinking. "Okay, um. You should probably get Wells Fargo to come pick that up. That's an awful lot of gold, son. Gotta be careful."

Gotta be careful. Blackie thought Hudson had no idea how dangerous things could get. He'd nearly gotten himself killed over a few ounces of gold. A wagonful of gold could start a war. Standing in that bank office as the last Cayuse, Blackie felt the sudden weight of what a war would mean. It was war, never-ending war, that had brought him to this point as the only living Cayuse. War never meant anything good for a Native.

"Can I trust Wells Fargo?"

Hudson chuckled. "Of course. They even got federal contracts. If you can't trust the federal government, who can ya trust?"

VII

To Blackie's surprise, the interaction with Wells Fargo was actually pretty uneventful. They first tried to bring a wagon up to his house but the trail was too small and rutted to get it up the mountain. Eventually, Blackie loaded up the saddle bags of his horses and walked them down the pass himself. That worked out better anyway. The Wells Fargo man had a general idea of where Blackie lived now, but he seemed like a professional enough guy. Blackie tipped him a handful of gold musket balls to keep his trail a secret. He didn't know if the man would actually do this, but it was all he could hope for.

Now, in the Look-See, Blackie and Debbie were toasting a successful transaction. In a few days, they would hear from the bank how much his gold was actually worth. But if it actually was as much as Blackie thought, it would be about $180,000. Blackie didn't even know how to conceive of that much money. The most cash he'd ever seen was about $500 when he'd had to carry a stack of greenbacks to the Sullivan's office while he was working for the ice company. That had felt like an unimaginable amount of money. Now, he could carry $500 worth of gold in his pockets without much effort.

Looking Glass placed two mugs of steam beer on the bar counter. Blackie thanked him and rolled him a glittering gold musket ball across the bar. Looking Glass slapped his hand down over the ball.

Looking Glass's mouth hung open. "Blackie, you serious?"

He nodded. "Just don't tell anybody."

Looking Glass nodded and dropped the gold in his vest pocket. "Thank you, Blackie. Thank you."

Looking Glass deserved it, Blackie figured. Hanging over the bar was the glimmering rifle that he'd used to defend his life and his gold. That rifle had saved him and afforded him the opportunity to live a truly exceptional life. It was all thanks to that rifle.

Blackie carried the two mugs over the table where Debbie was sitting and reading a book. It was a book Blackie had just bought for her. It was a black leather-clad book with gold script across the cover. The cover, in gold etching, said *Petticoat Rule*.

Blackie sat down and slid her mug towards her. Debbie looked over the top of her book. "Oh. Thank you."

Blackie sipped his beer, leaving a mustache of beer foam across his mouth. "Is it good? The book?"

"Oh, it's great." Her eyes lit up. "It's about a woman in France who is actually ruling France from behind the scenes."

Blackie nodded. "That's really something. You ever think a woman will run this country?"

Debbie laughed out loud, throwing her head back so Blackie could see the roof of her mouth. "Oh, honey, you're so naive. I think we've been running it all along." She paused and thought about it. "Except the Civil War. That was all you fellows."

Blackie shrugged and sipped his beer. "That wasn't Indians. We were just along for the ride."

"Fair enough."

The door to the saloon opened and a big-bellied man with a rapidly receding hairline pushed into the bar. It was Mr. Sullivan, the older of the Sullivan brothers who ran the ice company. He pushed past the table where Blackie and Debbie were sitting and bought a beer.

As he was walking back, he noticed Blackie and Debbie at the table. He shuffled over to them.

Blackie reached around and shook his hand. "How are you?"

"Blackie, Debbie, good to see you both."

Debbie looked up from her book and smiled. "Oh, I didn't even seen you there. I was lost in my book."

Sullivan laughed, "That's about what I'd expect. Care if I sit?"

Blackie pushed out the chair next to him with his foot. Sullivan plopped down and drank half of his beer in one gulp.

"Long day," he groaned.

Blackie took a few more sips of beer. "What's the problem?"

Sullivan chuckled, "Air conditioners. Air conditioners and refrigerators."

"Refrigerators?" Blackie asked.

Sullivan drank more of his beer until he was just down to the dregs. He looked over at the bar as if thinking he should have bought two beers at once. He drained the dregs after that, swallowing the bitter end of the steam beer.

"Yep. Mechanical refrigeration units. Keep everything right about 40 degrees. Meat, vegetables, everything."

Blackie nodded. "I know what they are. I just.. How are they a problem? Everybody seems to want one."

Sullivan nodded. "They sure do. That's not too good for a man who sells ice."

Blackie slowly started nodding. Finally, he understood why Sullivan was so upset. The unrelenting march of time, what some people simply called progress, always had its victims. A Cayuse knew that more than just about anybody. When the lands of Natives had been stripped, parceled, and sold, it was called progress as well. That kind of progress is the kind that leaves actual human beings bloodied and broken. This progress that was facing the Sullivans was one that never stopped and was difficult to even identify. There were no approaching armies with guns and horses. They weren't any batteries of cannons. No women and children running scared before the dust cloud of the American machine. This was just time creeping forward. Someone somewhere designed a way to keep things cold all year round with the help of electricity. They had made incredible scientific leaps that many hailed as progress. In a way, it was. More people than ever would be able to store food for longer. Businesses could save money which could drive their prices down -- Blackie noted that was unlikely, though. When costs went down, businesses he'd seen just seemed to pocket the extra money. They could be seen in their literal pockets, golden pocketwatches dangling that represented hoarding more of that progress.

It also left people behind; it always did, people like the Sullivans. What would Blackie have done if the refrigerator had been invented a few years ago? He had all the food and horses he could ever need; his bank account was stuffed to the gills with gold nuggets. But a few years ago, he'd been just an Indian running around with ice on his back. What would he have done if Sullivan had closed down then? Would he have gotten a new job? Who would have given him one? He didn't know how to build an air conditioner. He didn't even know where they were built -- probably somewhere in the East. That's the other way America drove people from their land. It moved in and chained them to the economy. It said the economy is a beast that needs to be fed. Then, they would move it. They would say the good jobs were somewhere else and you should go there. When you went, they built a new claw to the beast where you had left.

Blackie drained his beer. "I can save your company."

Debbie looked up over the top of her book again. She had a look of incredulity. "What?"

Sullivan echoed her. "What?"

"I can save your company," Blackie repeated. "Meet me at the office first thing tomorrow morning."

Debbie scrunched her eyebrows, "Honey, should we talk about this?"

"How can you save my company?"

Blackie shook his head at both of them. "I'm not doing it for you. I'm doing it for the next Indian kid who needs a job."

The next morning, Blackie came jogging out of the woods from his house with his hair flowing in the wind behind him. He didn't do too much of that lately. He'd been busy with his horses and with his farming. He didn't take enough time to just run. With his feet slapping in the dirt, silent as a wolf's, he felt like he was himself again. He hadn't run ice for the Sullivans in a few years, but he felt like that person again. He had his satchel on his hip, holding the strap tight with his hands so it didn't bang against his leg. It wasn't the heavy blocks of ice, but it did feel familiar. He was his old self again.

The city approached quickly as each smooth stride

covered great distances. A part of him wanted to be running forever. It was a thought that brought a smile to his
lips, but even he couldn't run forever. He wondered how far
he could run. He'd run himself to exhaustion by sprinting
hundreds of times, but he'd never set out a comfortable
pace and just seen how far he could go. Maybe that's what
he'd do -- just run for as long as he could and set up camp
wherever he fell. He'd done it with his father when he was
a kid but hadn't in quite some time.

He was at the front door of the Sullivan Ice Company
before he knew it, lost in his memories. He pushed into
the office and felt the oppressive weight of hot, stale air.
It was the way the office always felt in the summer -- like
dry kindling about to go up in flames. This was different,
though. So many businesses were trying to invest in some
kind of air conditioning system that it was starting to
stand out when they didn't.

The office was empty. It was empty a lot of the time
when he was working there, but usually you could find
stacks of papers filling ledgers. The Sullivans were usually pretty sloppy with their paperwork. They kind of let
business just roll in. They had a bad habit of letting people take out lines of credit with their company that never
quite added up. Blackie could specifically remember at
least one barber that had a cooler full of rotgut whiskey
and steam beer he used to keep for his customers. He
bought a block of ice every two days on credit. The man,
O'Shea was his name, was a man with a bright shock of
red hair that was starting to recede from his forehead and
a bushy mustache. Everybody liked O'Shea but he wasn't
very good with his money. When his business started suffering, the Sullivans let him get ice on a tab. He would pay
it off sometimes, but more often than not, the Sullivans
never saw a dime of the money they were owed. Their

business was pretty good and they were pretty nice guys, so they didn't worry too much about it. It was Debbie's job to worry.

She would go behind the Sullivans each night, grabbing up loose files and organizing them in file cabinets and drawers. The Sullivans would come in in the morning, complaining that they couldn't find anything. Debbie would chastise them that they had left their papers lying around and would never have found them again. One of them, the younger one usually, would counter that he would have found it right where he'd left it lying around if she hadn't gone fiddling with it.

There was none of that now. It was just empty halls and empty offices. Blackie walked through the halls barefoot, his feet padding softly on the wooden floor. The gold rocks in his bag jangled slightly in their metal can.

"Sullivan?" He called out.

The younger Sullivan, a little bit shorter and skinnier than his brother, stepped out of an office. He was sweaty, his tie pulled loose and his hair swept back with salty sweat. He looked shocked to see Blackie.

"Oh, Blackie. Hey. Haven't seen you in a while."

Blackie shook his hand, "I told your brother I was coming by."

The younger Sullivan waved Blackie into his office. The office was almost completely bare. The walls were stripped and the cabinets were open. Everything was in a heap of wooden crates scattered around the floor. There were files, a lantern, some keepsakes, inkpens, and everything else you would need to run a business.

"Just packing up the office," he said.

Sullivan hustled back and forth, stacking things into the wooden boxes.

Blackie asked, "Your brother didn't tell you?"

Sullivan didn't look up from his packing. He replied, "Tell me what?"

Blackie fished around in his bag and pulled out a coffee can stuffed to the rim with golden musket balls. The musket balls, glimmer balls of pure gold, clanged around and one of them dropped to the floor. It rolled across the wooden floor towards Sullivan. Sullivan leaned down and picked it up. His eyes grew twice as big.

His mouth fell open. "Is this?"

Blackie shoved the entire coffee can into his chest. "Pure gold."

Sullivan took the coffee can, cradling it like a baby. He stared down in it with his eyes wide. He didn't say anything, just looked at it.

Blackie said, "Should be about seven or eight pounds. Is that enough to buy air conditioners?"

Sullivan just nodded. He was still speechless.

Blackie sighed. "Oh good. I have more if you need it."

"Blackie, where'd you get this?"

Blackie shrugged. "I have a creek. I wanted to thank you guys for helping me."

"Helping you? We just gave you a job. We made you lug around all that damn ice."

Blackie clapped Sullivan on the shoulder. "You don't know what that means to a Cayuse. Not a lot of folks out here would even give a guy like me a chance."

Blackie turned to leave.

"Wait," Sullivan called after him. "How can we ever repay you?"

Blackie shrugged. "I wouldn't mind an air conditioner." Just like that he was off, jogging back through the hallway.

Sullivan rushed out into the hallway. "Wait! At least let me buy you a drink."

Blackie laughed. "Sure thing."

The Look-See was pretty empty except for a few employees from the Sullivan Ice Company. There were about eight of them in all. They would need to change the name from the Sullivan Ice Company to something new. Maybe the Sullivan Refrigeration Company. In the few months since Blackie had given them a coffee can full of 1.5 oz. gold balls, they'd been able to pay the past due rent on their office and keep it open. Then, they'd been able to buy a couple of air conditioning units from a railroad company that had gone belly up.

The company, The Falling Rock Railroad Company, had been hired out of Missouri to connect St. Louis to Chicago. As it turned out, the owner of the company was actually just a talented liar. He had convinced the governors of Missouri and Illinois that he could do the job for a staggeringly low sum of money. The entire time he'd been squirreling the money away in an account in Prussia. His scheme had been simple but brutally effective. He rounded all of his expenses up when he reported the prices to his investors. He'd then rounded down all of the salaries when he paid his employees. He bought the supplies from a company owned by his brother in California. They took the difference, pocketed all the proceeds, and were in Prussia before anybody was any the wiser. The governments of Illinois and Missouri decided to sell off the railroad and all of its supplies to try and take the sting out of their losses. So, for just a few gold balls, the Sullivans owned a few air conditioners for rail cars, and their business was on its feet.

The first thing they did was hire some more employees. They had a line on a supplier for air conditioners in Santa Fe, New Mexico. They were expanding pretty rapidly, and that had brought all of them to the Look-See to celebrate. The ink was barely dry on the contract in Santa Fe, and the paperwork hadn't even made it all the way through the Postal Service, but they were ready for some good news.

Blackie and Debbie sat at a table with both Sullivan brothers, drinking cold steam beer and chasing back drams of whiskey. The older Sullivan lifted up his metal whiskey cup and held it over the table.

"To Blackie and to random good deeds."

Debbie cheered loudest and clacked her cup against his cup.

Blackie nudged her with his elbow. "And just think, you were against me helping them out."

Debbie frowned. "I wasn't against you helping them. I was against you making decisions with boatloads of gold without asking me. Big difference."

"When do I ever make money decisions?"

"When you decide to give it away, apparently," she replied and laughed.

Everyone at the table laughed.

A young kid walked up to the table. He was skinny in the way boys were when they were raised out on the hard edge of the frontier. He had skinny cheeks and broad shoulders that he would one day grow into if he got a steady diet of food. Until then, he'd look like somebody had stretched not enough boy over too much skeleton. His hair was a messy tangle of floppy curls that bounced on his head. He looked something like Blackie when he was a kid. He could have been white, but it was just as likely he wasn't. His skin was the muddy clay color that comes from exposure to the sun or Native blood.

Sullivan held a drink out to the kid. He reached for it, then Sullivan pulled it back. He eyed the kid skeptically "Wait, how old are you?"

The kid shrugged. "Um, eighteen?"

Sullivan pushed the beer into the boy's hands. "That wasn't even the least bit convincing."

The boy smiled and took the beer. He drank it greedily then pulled his face back. He made a sour face. "You guys drink this stuff?"

Sullivan laughed, "The third one tastes a lot better."

The kid's eyes settled on Blackie. He studied Blackie for a minute as the Cayuse nursed his beer. The kid spoke in almost a reverential whisper.

"You're Blackie, aren't you?" The kid asked.

Blackie nodded. "Yep."

The kid set his beer down on the table and held out his hand. Blackie shook his hand. Blackie tried to pull his hand back but the boy held onto it.

"Is it true?" He asked in a near-whisper?

Blackie scrunched up his brow. "Is what true?"

The kid replied, "Are you the fastest man in the world?"

Blackie frowned again and shook his head slightly. He didn't seem to understand the question.

The boy rephrased, "Did you beat the Olympian? The white guy?"

Blackie smiled. "Oh, I haven't even thought about that for years. It wasn't really like that."

The kid reached back to a different table and grabbed a chair. He dragged the chair across the floor with a scraping whine of the legs against the wooden floor. "What was it like?"

VIII

Four Years Earlier

John Larson had a car. That was the first thing most people in Walla Walla notice. It was a Ford Model C that had rolled off the assembly line in Detroit not even a full year earlier. The car, solid black, was covered in a spray of brown dust from the road into Walla Walla. It bumped and bounced as the skinny tires navigated the rocky dirt road. A plume of dust chased after the car as it rumbled into town. The engine growled and sputtered as it rolled.

Eventually, the car came to a stop outside of the Post Office with a squeal of the brakes. The door swung open and John Larson jumped out. He was a skinny man with long legs and a shock of bright, blond hair that gleamed in the noonday sun. He wore a three-piece suit, black and white pinstripes, with a matching vest; it was the kind of thing you didn't see much in Walla Walla. The frontier town was the sort of hardscrabble place where men wore canvas pants and tall boots, not loafers and tailored suits.

Squinting against the sun, Larson reached back into his car and grabbed a dark fedora off the bench seat. He plopped the hat onto his head and walked into the post office.

The air in the post office was hot and stale. The sunlight battering through the dirty windows diffused in dusty lines across the floor. He walked up to the counter where the postal worker was a short man with a big belly. He was sipping lemonade from a dirty glass and reading a newspaper. Larson walked up and stood at the counter. The postal worker looked over, studied him up and down and went back to reading.

Larson cleared his throat. "Excuse me."

His voice was high-pitched and soft with the lilting accent of Northern England. The postal worker laughed.

"The British are coming," he chuckled.

Larson straightened up, adjusting his tie. "My name is Sir John Charles Larson."

"Good for you," the man replied.

Larson went on. "...and I am here to promote the Olympic Games this year. I will be participating as an athlete representing the United Kingdom of Great Britain and Ireland."

The man replied, "Well, good luck to you."

Larson rolled his eyes, but tried to keep his composure. "As a means of promotion, I would like to speak with the best athlete in town. The fastest man in this... city."

The Postal Worker didn't even look up. "You're looking for Blackie Sullivan. Injun fella runs around here all day long."

"And where can I find this Mr. Sullivan?"

The employee shrugged. "Look for a redskin running around with ice on his back. There's only the one."

"Thank you, sir." Larson turned to leave. The man just sort of grunted in response but Larson was already out the door.

He asked around town for Blackie for a while. He couldn't get a straight answer about where the man might be, but everyone did agree that he was probably the fastest man in Walla Walla. They told stories that were frankly unbelievable.

Larson walked into the dusty bar called the Look-See. He sat down at the bar and placed his hat on the stool next to him.

"My name is Sir John Charles Larson," he told the bartender.

The bartender shook his hand and said, "My name is Looking Glass."

Larson looked all around the bar. It was mostly empty except for two guys sitting at a table by the window. The tables were simple, sturdy wood in need of a new coat of varnish. The bar was unimpressive, and the stools were rough and unpadded. It was the kind of pub he wouldn't be caught dead in back in England. But America had different standards, he supposed. Especially out here on this rough frontier. Everything seemed to be coated in a layer of dust.

Everything except a rifle that hung over the bar. It looked to be cleaned meticulously with an oily rag. The light glimmered off the shimmering metal and the brass inlays. The brass gleamed like gold, displaying what looked like two men on horses. It was the only nice thing in the bar from what Larson could see.

"I'm looking for Blackie Sullivan," he said.

The man behind the counter eyed him suspiciously. He frowned at him. "What's he to you?"

Larson explained who he was. He explained that he was there to race the fastest man in Walla Walla.

Two of the men overheard him talking.

"I know where you can find Blackie," he said. "We're

a little fond of placing a bet or two on how quick he can get from place to place. Once seen him run 'bout a mile in what had to be five minutes tops."

Larson chuckled and rolled his eyes. "Where can I find this super human?"

The man sucked his teeth and shrugged. "I don't know that I feel comfortable telling you. I'd much rather tell President George Washington."

Larson scrunched up his face. The man rubbed his thumb against his fingers. Money. He wanted money. Larson groaned and rolled his eyes.

He pulled a folded one dollar silver certificate out his vest pocket and handed it to the man. The man perked up in a hurry.

"The name's King Roger. Blackie ought to be coming by here in about a half-hour. If he's on schedule. He's always on schedule."

═══════════════

They marked the route in Larson's car. It was a two mile loop through town that would take them past most of the landmarks in Walla Walla and finish back at the Look-See. The next day, early in the morning, he jogged into the Look-See. The Sullivans had offered him the day off work since he was going to be racing John Larson, but he insisted that they race early in the morning so he could still make his deliveries on time. So, before the sun had even broken over the treeline, he was running into the Look-See barefoot and shirtless. He already had a sheen of sweat glistening across his skin.

The sun wasn't up yet but it was already brutally hot in Walla Walla. It was what his father used to call oppressively hot. He was shocked when he jogged into the bar. It was practically empty every time he went in there, and that's what he expected again. That wasn't the case, though. The bar was stuffed with the people of Walla Walla, so close together that they had to stand shoulder to shoulder. The room was hot like breath and smelled like sweat. The people didn't even really notice him walk in. The room felt a lot like some barns Blackie had been in. He didn't spend much time in barns when he was younger. The Cayuse had raised their horses out in the open. They raised some of the best horses this side of the Mississippi River, so they were apparently onto something.

Blackie tried to push through the crowd of people. They started to murmur and mumble as he was making his way up to the bar. There weren't many Natives in Walla Walla; pretty much everyone instantly recognized Blackie. He walked through the crowd and they whispered as he passed; it was bizarre. They were treating him like he was some kind of important figure. Blackie was uncomfortable with the notion. Then he considered another possibility; maybe they weren't being reverential, but instead were worried for him. They were worried that he was about to be embarrassed and make their town an embarrassment as well. They'd never seen a professional runner before. They knew that Blackie was fast, but that was only when compared to other people in Walla Walla. What if this professional runner from England was actually the fastest man in the world as he claimed? How badly would Blackie get beaten?

There was one man who didn't doubt for a second Blackie would win. That was the smiling drunk, King Roger. He stumbled up to Blackie with a beer in hand. It was already halfway gone and from the way he was grinning, it wasn't his first one. The sun wasn't even up yet.

"You're going to pass out before the sun even rises," Blackie said.

King Roger's head lolled back and forth. "Not a chance, Blackie. I'm gonna watch you win and collect a whole buncha money. Believe you me."

"What if I lose?" Blackie asked.

King Roger stood there for a minute with his face all scrunched up. He looked like he was trying to even process what those words meant, as if Blackie were speaking some kind of foreign language.

"What do you mean?" He asked.

Blackie shrugged. "What if this guy is faster than me?"

King Roger lazily shoved Blackie on the shoulder. "Ain't nobody faster than my man Blackie. Don't you worry about that at all."

Blackie got up to the bar where Looking Glass was sliding drinks to customers. He shoved the beers down the bar and watched them slide into waiting hands. Foamy beer sloshed all over the bar.

He smiled and waved at Blackie as the Cayuse man leaned against the wood. "Business is pretty good today, eh Looking Glass?"

Looking Glass laughed. "I might close up before the sun even rises today. This is great."

The bar got quiet, as if someone had pulled the needle off a phonograph. Blackie looked around for what had changed. The crowd of people slid to the side and he was face to face across the bar with Sir John Charles Larson. Larson was wearing a pair of thin cotton shorts that cut off above his knee, a sleeveless shirt so thin you could see his chest through the fabric, and a wide-brimmed hat that cast a shadow on his face. He walked towards Blackie, his feet padding silently across the wooden floor. He was wearing a pair of shoes like Blackie had never seen before. They were thin and form-fitting to his foot. They were made of a thin leather, thinner than even a belt. The soles were tan rubber that landed softly on the wooden floor without a sound. They laced up the front so they kept tight to his feet.

Blackie looked down at his own bare feet, dirty from the Walla Walla dust. The two of them shook hands. Larson looked down at Blackie's feet and the corner of his top lip curled upwards just slightly with disgust. He straightened his face.

"I'm not much of a gambling man, Mr. Sullivan," he said. "I find it puts me at ill humor. But I do fancy a wager before a footrace. All the better to enhance the competition, wouldn't you say?"

Blackie shrugged. "I guess so."

Larson smiled, "Very well. I am willing to wager this very pair of shoes on my feet. They are bespoke shoes made by a cobbler in Oregon. Nary a sewing machine has touched these shoes."

Blackie nodded. "They're very nice shoes, but uh, I have nothing to bet. Sorry."

Looking Glass chimed in from behind the bar. "Nonsense. You can bet my rifle. Lewis and Clark carried this thing you know."

Larson frowned. "Which one?"

Looking Glass frowned back, "Which one what?"

Larson replied, "Lewis or Clark?"

Looking Glass laughed. "You know, I've never really thought to wonder about that. Either way, it's pretty valuable. Ain't gonna ever be another one like it unless Teddy Roosevelt buys some more America from the French."

Blackie shook his head. "I can't ask you to do that, Looking Glass. That thing is priceless. You can't afford to lose it."

Looking Glass gave him a serious look. "Then don't lose."

Larson and Blackie shook hands. "I have always wanted a rifle. You Americans are positively obsessed with them. I'd love to fit in."

They approached the starting line, a line in the dirt someone had dragged with his toe. Blackie scooted his bare toes up to the line. Larson pushed his leather shoe up to the line as well, crouching and leaning forward. He bent his arms at right angles to mimic running. If this were a photo, you might be forgiven for thinking he was already running. Blackie stood there next to him, with his back straight and his hair flapping in the wind. He wiggled his toes in the dirt, working out a cramp that had settled in. He told himself it was just nerves. He didn't want to lose Looking Glass's gun. That was his only real concern.

Larson looked over at Blackie who had yet to take a starting crouch. The man narrowed his eyes. "If you have a mind to intimidate, sir, I'll tell you that it's futile."

Blackie looked confused but didn't say anything. He was too busy looking out at the crowds lining the street. It looked like just about everybody in Walla Walla had come out to see this. There was a photographer from the newspaper standing on the porch balcony of a hotel with his camera shutter clicking. It was a Brownie, the kind of camera that people could buy in the general store. It wasn't much for a newspaper reporter but Walla Walla in 1906 wasn't a very prosperous town. The newspaper got by with what they could afford. There wasn't anyone from the farther away papers in the state. Just the one man in the wide-brimmed hat, trying to capture a moment for his paper.

There were men and women standing all alongside the street. They fidgeted in the hot sun. In the time it had taken to get everybody out to the route, the sun had started its climb through the sky. The women wore floppy sun hats and light-colored dresses to shield them from the sun. The men were dressed in the uniforms of their occupation -- bankers wore simple dark-colored suits, sweating through the wool and dabbing their foreheads with handkerchiefs. The cowboys and cattle ranchers wore canvas pants and shirts unbuttoned to the navel, all of them slick with sweat. One man stood out to Blackie as he stood on the sidelines. He was taller than most of the other people in Walla Walla, and he was the only person darker than Blackie. From afar, he looked like he could be Blackie's father actually.

The man, his bald head shimmering with sweat, wore a pair of denim overalls that looked like they'd been through several hundred miles of hard road. He was a teamster. Blackie could see that; you could tell a teamster by the easy, authoritative way they carried themselves. Like they were always in charge but never uneasy. He wasn't Blackie's father and as the Cayuse man stared at him, he could see notable differences. This man was taller and broader at the shoulders than Blackie's father. And from the way the light glinted off his skin, this man was black and not Cayuse. Probably the son of slaves, a man who left the South looking for more opportunity. He'd left the South that bore black bodies swinging from trees like bloated fruit for the Northwest where he wasn't allowed. There weren't enough black people in Walla Walla to put racial segregation into law but he knew where he wasn't welcome. They were the same places Blackie wasn't welcome.

Debbie Wagner walked out into the middle of the street about ten yards away from Blackie and Larson. She carried a thin, white umbrella trimmed with lace that matched her lacy dress dragging through the dirt. She carried a revolver in her hand -- an 1847 Walker Colt. The same kind of pistol General Walker had invented with Samuel Colt because he wanted a pistol deadlier at close range. He used them in the Mexican-American War to help steal Texas from Mexico and preserve the right to own slaves. It was a weapon of plunder, the kind the Cayuse knew too well.

The gun, the most powerful handgun ever produced at the time, was as long as Debbie's forearm and probably twice as heavy. She lifted the pistol into the air above her head, pointing it straight up.

Before she pulled the trigger, the teamster who looked like Blackie's father cupped his hands beside his mouth and shouted, "Make us proud, Blackie!"

Blackie didn't know who "us" might refer to. It could be the townspeople of Walla Walla who were tired of hearing about the majesty in Oregon in the same breath as disrespect for their arid town. But Blackie thought it was something else. Looking at the teamster in the battered denim, Blackie knew who he meant. He knew who "us" was. It was the two dark faces in the sea of white ones. It was the ruddy-skinned man with the long black hair standing next to the English gentleman and his fancy shoes. "Us" was the people who weren't supposed to be in Walla Walla.

At that moment, Blackie wanted to win for himself for the first time. He'd wanted to keep Looking Glass's gun, and he liked to run. That's why he'd agreed. But now, he thought he had to win for himself. He needed to prove that white men were no better than anyone else. Men were just men. Some were brown and some were white, but they were just men. He looked over at Sir John Charles Larson crouching and eagle-eyeing Debbie, waiting for her to shoot the starting gun.

Some of those brown men, Blackie thought, could be faster than any white man had ever been.

The Walker Colt thundered in Debbie's hand, blowing a plume of black smoke into the air. Debbie looked shocked by the noise and the thudding power of the Walker. At the sound of the gun, a cheer went up from the crowd.

Larson jumped out in front at the sound of the gun, not hesitating. Blackie flinched at the boom of the pistol. By the time he shoved forward and took his first stride, Larson was three strides ahead. A collective groan went up from the people in the crowd.

The sun gleamed against Larson's white skin as sweat glazed a sheen across his arms. Blackie didn't know how to race the way Larson did. Larson was a strategist; he knew how it felt to run at his goal pace. He knew how to run a two-mile race. He would jump out in front and attempt to hold close to Blackie for the first three-fourths of the race. At the last half-mile, he would turn up the intensity and try to put it away.

That wasn't the way Blackie ran. He didn't deliver ice by pacing himself and planning to deliver his last deliveries the fastest. He brought the same intensity to each and every delivery. The Sullivan brothers offered a service to the businesses in Walla Walla, and they offered the same service to each and every business. That was what the people expected from the Sullivan brothers and from Blackie. It was the only thing he knew.

Blackie stretched his legs as he ran, the muscles in his legs relaxing. He fell into a groove that usually came whenever he ran. He didn't hear the crowds of people shouting. They could have been shouting for Blackie or for Larson; it didn't matter to him. All Blackie could hear was the sound of blood rushing through his ears and his feet pitter-pattering against the ground. The ground was still warm from the day before, and the road was rough and jagged. The uneven stones jutted up in different directions; not a single step was smooth. Blackie knew these roads, though. The roads knew him.

His feet, bare and dusty, were rough and calloused. The pads of his feet were tough like shoe leather but soft like rubber. He brought each foot down on the balls of the feet and rolled his ankle until his toes splayed against the ground. His knees bent to absorb the shock and spring him forward. Each step was like a cobra striking. His knees bent and gathered up energy then uncoiled. He focused on his own body more than even looking forward. He kept his eyes on the ground to ensure that he didn't miss a step on the uneven, craggy road. Walla Walla was known for a lot of things but the quality of its roads wasn't one.

Because he was keeping his eyes on the ground, Blackie didn't see himself creeping up on Larson. He knew that Larson was up ahead of him but not much more than that. He didn't know how far Larson was or how close. In a sense, it didn't matter to Blackie. He wanted to win; that much was obvious. The look he'd shared with the teamster before the gun went off was enough to spur him forward but it didn't actually matter where Sir Larson was. Blackie had to run his race. There was nothing about Larson being ahead of him that could change anything about that. So, Blackie kept his head down. He kept his eyes on the ground, carefully picking his steps. He concentrated on turning his legs over as quickly as he could.

He'd developed a habit, a tactic of the mind, while he was delivering ice. He would imagine his legs like a horse's legs. Horses didn't take one step then the next, the way it might look like a person runs on his two legs. A horse moved its entire body in concert. Its hind legs and fore legs moved in unison to create a symphony of controlled motion. Blackie had only ever caught glimpses of himself running in the windows of storefronts but he knew that he didn't look like a horse when he was running, but he felt like one. He imagined a horse drawing deep breaths into its chest and exhaling slowly. Sometimes, his hair did feel like a mane, though. He and horses had that in common.

He often thought his musing about being a horse had started when he began delivering ice for a living as a way to cope with the monotony and the stress. But that wasn't true. He'd first started imagining himself in this way when he was still a little boy, when there had been more Cayuse. His father would take him out with some of the other men and older boys to take care of the horses or to race the horses. Only the oldest boys got to actually race in the horse races, so Blackie and some of the young ones would run alongside the horses that were racing. They'd line up next to the marked-off horse race path and crouch like cobras. When the gun went off, the kids would race each other alongside the older boys racing their horses.

The little boys thought they were racing each other but Blackie always thought he was racing the horses. Most boys fell behind quickly, choking on the clouds of dust kicked up by the horses. Blackie lasted longer, though. He learned that if you took off fast enough, you could actually outrun the horses for a little while. They eventually raced past him, but for a few yards, for a few long seconds, he was winning. He never got fast enough to beat them, but he got close a few times.

That's how he felt now. He wasn't racing Sir John Charles Larson, the British man running for Oregon. He was racing those horses all over again. He was a little kid again racing those horses. He could see them in his mind. He could hear the thundering pattering of their hooves. He could feel the dust scratching in his throat. He looked up and he wasn't in the dusty meadow of his youth racing horses. He was in Walla Walla racing Sir John Charles Larson, and they were next to each other.

He was a half-step behind Larson's right shoulder. The white man's shoulders were pumping furiously, his arms swinging back and forth in tight jabs. His legs turned over like pistons. They weren't the fluid, graceful movements of a horse; they were the strong, powerful motions of a man who thought of running as fighting. Larson thought of running as an adversarial showdown. A man like Larson fought against the ground, fought against his body, fought against his own fatigue to scratch and claw every bit of speed he could find. His face was pained as he ran. His mouth was open in a kind of grimace or growl, sucking wind as he ran.

Blackie, on the other hand, was relaxed and calm. His hair flew loosely behind him. His arms moved back and forth in tight circles in time with his legs. Right arm, left leg. Left arm, right leg. He kept perfect balance as he ran, not rocking side to side or up and down. When he was carrying the blocks of ice, he couldn't sway too much side to side or he'd come unbalanced and the ice would drag him down. If he moved up and down, the ice would bang against his back. Instead, he developed a smoother way of running. He didn't slap the ground with his feet to push himself forward. He pawed at the ground as lightly as he could with each step. He was almost silent when he was running. Larson thundered like a buffalo.

Just like that, Blackie was passing Larson. The Englishman, sweat glimmering against his white skin, looked to his right as the Cayuse passed. His mouth was open, to breathe not in shock, but it could have been either. His eyes stretched wide as Blackie passed him. Blackie glanced at Larson as he passed. It felt like passing those horses when he was a little kid. Blackie saw surprise on Larson's face. He couldn't tell if it was surprise that a Cayuse was passing him, surprise that anyone was passing him, or just surprise at the easy smile on Blackie's face. The easy look on his face didn't mean that he wasn't hurting. Blackie was definitely feeling the burn starting to creep into his lungs as he was running. Each breath he took felt just a little less satisfying than the last and he was starting to have trouble pushing air out of his lungs fast enough. That was the real danger when sprinting like this. Getting air into your lungs isn't an issue. Getting air out gets harder and harder.

So, Blackie was definitely feeling pain clutching his chest, but he wasn't worried about it. Pain was like any other situation. Just because he was in pain didn't mean he gave in to it. He went to work when he was angry, he smiled when he was sad, and he could run when he was in pain.

Maybe that wasn't what Larson was looking at at all. Maybe Larson noticed a man who had never raced before in his life, sprinting all out in the first half of the race. Maybe he thought Blackie was some uncultured Indian who had no idea how to properly race. Blackie didn't have any idea about racing; that much was true. He knew about running, though, and he never did that halfway. He didn't think about it too long because he was past Larson quickly. He could hear the man struggling behind him, breathing hard and stomping his feet but he couldn't see him. Blackie wouldn't see Larson's back again for the entire race.

The race turned at the Steamed Clam, the bar where the Butcher met with his goons to plot Blackie's murder. He didn't know it at the time but that bar was going to change his life in more than one way. At the time, all he knew was that it was that the road curved after the Steamed Clam and he was supposed to follow it. He leaned into the turn with his whole body, trying to keep his balance without losing any speed. As he rounded the turn, he could see Larson out of the corner of his eye. Larson was just entering the turn. He looked haggard and tired earlier. Now, he looked something else: angry. He looked like a man who was mad at the world and honestly, he looked angry at Blackie.

Blackie didn't really think much of it because as soon as he took his eyes off the road to look at Larson, his foot landed on a rock. The rock wasn't big -- only about the size of a musket ball. Blackie's foot landed on it and it sent a shock of hot pain through his foot like a knife. Blackie felt his knee go weak and he stumbled forward. The pain was sharp enough that the world rocked a little bit and the sunlight grew blinding. He didn't see stars -- that was a myth about pain -- he saw hot white light shoot into his vision and his breath hitched. He focused on letting his breath out slowly and regaining his footing.

He'd lost his rhythm, though. So much of running is about rhythm. If you can slip into a good flow, you can block out the pain of the rain. Now, his breath and his feet were scrambling wildly. He gasped a few times, trying to get his breathing under control. He stumbled forward, jabbing his toe into the ground. He felt his toenail rip off his foot and a gush of blood wet the ground. That fresh pain worked through his foot again. As Blackie finally came out of the turn, gasping and missing a toenail, he saw Larson coming on strong. The stumble had cost him maybe two seconds, but in running, that was enough.

The look on Larson's face had shifted from one of anger or disbelief to a kind of raging determination. It was as if his mouth was locked in a growl with his teeth clenched. It was the kind of look Blackie recognized from angry dogs.

Now shoulder to shoulder, they fell into a kind of rhythm together. Their arms pumped in time and their feet hit the ground simultaneously. Blackie's steps were a light pitter patter that barely made a sound. He left only droplets of blood from his toe where he ran. His arms moved in tiny circles. Larson's feet slapped the ground with the thundering pounding of his rubber soled shoes.

As quickly as they'd pulled even, Blackie was pulling away again. He didn't notice Larson fading behind him. He kept his eyes on the ground in front of him and the pain that was spiking through his foot. He did a quick diagnostic of his body. His lungs were burning but he was keeping his breathing under control. He didn't know how much longer he could run; it had been a long time since he'd run himself to exhaustion. His dad used to call it running himself into the ground.

A lot of the Cayuse used the same phrase. It came from the process of running a horse for too long. The Cayuse were master horse riders known for raising incredibly quick horses of all different breeds. Because of their mastery of horseflesh, they were often hired as scouts and mail couriers. The post office always wanted the Cayuse to whip their horses harder, ride them longer, push them faster. They wouldn't do it but many of the white couriers did. They would run their horses until they collapsed. That was running a horse into the ground.

Blackie hadn't run himself into the ground since he was a kid, but he thought he might be headed that direction this time. His lungs were burning, slow to expand and contract. He couldn't seem to get enough air out of his lungs to get new air in. His legs were burning too, throbbing in time with his footfalls and the pain in his bloody toe. He turned a corner and sprinted towards what had to be the finish. There was a stripe of paint dragged across the ground through the dust.

As fast as he ran, he didn't think it was getting any closer. The finish line just bounced in the distance at what looked like a fixed location. That's when Blackie felt it. He felt the edges of his vision starting to darken. Tiny blasts of starlight bounced through his vision. The edges of his vision were starting to gray out and tunnel down. Looking forward, he could only see the finish line in the distance through a dark tunnel. He was starting to feel like he was floating above his own body. As the darkness was starting to creep into his sight, he remembered that he wasn't actually remembering things properly. He had run himself into the ground before.

A few years ago, he'd been working a double shift for the Sullivan brothers. It was unseasonably warm; the kind of September or October that white people called Indian summer. He didn't know why they called it that because he suffered through the summer just as much as any white person. He'd been delivering the ice during his second half of the shift. He'd felt the edges creeping in and the world losing its color. The color drained from the world and from his face. He woke up a few minutes later with his knees and his forehead scraped bloody. He was on the ground, pinned under a heavy block of ice. Blood ran down his face and pain thundered in his head. He'd had a thundering headache for about a week after that. He'd been dizzy and tired, frequently having to take a seat during his shift or even vomiting in the street. He suspected what he had was what doctors called shaking of the brain or a concussion. That's where he figured he was heading now. He was going to wake up bloody on the pavement with all of Walla Walla laughing at him.

All of Walla Walla except the teamster with the dark skin and the shimmering bald head. No, he wasn't going to pass out. He wasn't going to let the heat, the town, or the rich man from England beat him. He was going to win for himself and for the teamster with the bald head. He didn't know where Larson was. For all he knew, Larson was right off his shoulder in the blackness that edged out his vision.

Finally, the finish line looked close enough for Blackie to reach out and touch. He kept his eyes on the ground at his feet and the finish line in front of him. The blackness grew and grew. He felt himself getting cold. Why was he so cold? The temperature had been steadily climbing for hours, but he was getting colder and colder. His finger-tips began to tingle. His tongue was swollen and dry in his mouth. He couldn't even breathe around his cottony tongue. He tried to inhale but nothing happened. His lungs seized as if a drawstring had been pulled. He saw the finish line at his feet. The blackness grabbed Blackie.

＝＝＝＝＝＝

Blackie opened his eyes expecting to feel a fifty pound block of ice crushing into his spine. He didn't. He felt a hand shaking him. It was a nervous frantic shake. The noise was deafening. Looking around, he saw clusters of feet, bare feet, feet in boots, the shoes of bank managers, cattle ropers, and a teamster. He saw the dusty boots of a teamster scuffed and dirty. He lifted his head off the ground and saw the smiling face of Debbie Wagner. She was biting her lip and shaking his shoulder.

"Blackie. Blackie," she said, "Wake up."

Blackie blinked a few times. "I'm awake. I'm awake."

"Are you okay?"

Blackie rolled over onto his back. He tried to sit up on his hands but his head swam. Hot agony shot through his head and his stomach roiled. His mouth was full of liquid. A mouthful of spit that tasted like copper. He spat into the dirt next to him. A stream of syrupy red blood splattered into the dust. He wiped his mouth on his forearm.

His vision was doubled and blurry. Everything was hazy and distant. The sun beat down on him and stabbed him in the eyes. He laid back down, the back of his head hitting the pavement a little more roughly than he'd intended.

Larson, the British man, stood over Blackie who shielded his eyes with his hands. Larson leaned over, a drop of sweat from his chin dripped and plopped onto Blackie's forehead. Blackie didn't even bother wiping it off. He just winced at the hot salty drop.

Larson frowned, almost growling. "I suspect I owe you a pair of shoes."

Blackie groaned. "Huh?"

Debbie smiled. "You won, Blackie. You won."

"Won what? The race?"

Debbie laughed. "Yes, silly. The race."

Debbie held a pocket watch up in front of his face. His eyes couldn't focus. He just shook his head.

Debbie said, "Eight minutes and four seconds. That's a record."

Blackie nodded. "Well, of course it's a record. I've never run it before."

Debbie punched him lightly in the arm. "No. A *world* record."

Blackie frowned. "Oh, I didn't know they kept track of that sort of thing."

A strong, muscled arm extended down towards Blackie. It was the sweaty arm of the teamster in the overalls. Blackie took his hand; it was like grabbing steel. The teamster hoisted Blackie to his feet. Blackie stumbled and tipped into the man's arms.

He used his strong arms to hold Blackie up by his shoulders. Blackie, unsteady on his feet, wobbled as the teamster held him up.

The man gently shook Blackie. "You're the fastest man in the world. How's it feel?"

Blackie frowned as if he was thinking about it. He turned his face to the side and streamed vomit onto the ground. The hot vomit splattered against the ground. Blackie coughed and spat again. The teamster frowned at the acrid smell of the vomit.

The teamster laughed. "You don't seem very excited."

Blackie just shrugged. "I don't feel so good."

Larson was cordial when he presented Blackie with his pair of leather shoes with the rubber soles. He handed them to Blackie and offered some kind words. He didn't go as far as offering Blackie a spot to train with him on any of his teams or even mention going to the election. Blackie didn't think much about it, but Debbie was angry on his behalf. Debbie tried to press Blackie, telling him that Larson was scared of Blackie. He didn't want anyone to know that Blackie had set a world record. Blackie didn't really understand why anyone would be embarrassed about not winning a race. It was only one race in a dusty frontier town. Who could possibly be so worried about one race?

Blackie tossed the shoes in his hands. They were heavy and stiff. His bloody toe still throbbed. Even after a few hours of sitting in the Look-See and nursing his toe. These shoes would have prevented him from hurting his toe, but at what cost? They were inflexible, heavy, and awkward. Blackie didn't know how much they cost but they looked and felt expensive. The leather was supple and well-oiled. The rubber was soft and forgiving. He shrugged and tossed them in a trash can as he walked away from the Look-See.

Debbie was shocked. "Don't you want to keep those? They seem very nice."

Blackie shrugged. "There's nothing wrong with my feet right now."

Larson went on to win Olympic events, the newspaper said. Blackie read about it one day before work.

IX

2008

The Cross family car was only a few miles outside of Umatilla, Oregon when the gas light came on. The little yellow light beamed and dinged a few times to let John Charles Cross know that his car was getting dangerously low on gas. The economy had been sputtering and faltering for months by now and he had gotten into the habit of driving until the light came on. It wasn't the best practice for his gas tank -- he'd heard somewhere if you let the gas get too low, it could stir up muck from the bottom of the gas tank and clog up your fuel lines. He didn't know if there was much truth to that, but he didn't have much of a choice.

His son, John Jr, was about to become an Oregon Duck. He had a partial scholarship because he was pretty quick at the 3200 meters -- an event they usually called the 2-mile even though that wasn't completely accurate. He had a partial scholarship but the price of tuition, dorm, and books was more than the Cross family could easily shoulder. So, he let the gas tank empty as much as possible before pouring his money into the tank. They'd crossed the

Columbia River only a few miles back and the air coming off the river was still cool and damp.

It was August, so the temperature was rising pretty quickly. They'd been driving for a few hours to get to Eugene. By the time they'd stopped for gas, the sun was high and hot in the sky. The only saving grace was the cool breeze coming off the river. In the distance, the Blue Mountains rose into the sky -- green and bright at the base and fading into the hazy blue sky near the clouds. The tip of the peaks were indistinct and misty.

John Cross steered his car off the interstate and cruised to a stop next to a gas station pump. The gas station had a fresh coat of crimson and yellow paint on the canopy. In crimson, the sign over the gas station proclaimed it the Core of Discovery Fuel and Snacks.

John stepped out of the car and smoothed his pants. He stretched his legs and reached up high over his head to stretch his back. John Jr. bounced out of the car with the energy of a teenager and bounded into the gas station.

John's wife and John Jr.'s mother, Emily, stayed in the car. She was flipping through the course catalog for the University of Oregon, engrossed in the wide array of electives. She thumbed through a few pages depicting a multiethnic group of students smiling and laughing. They were digging in a muddy field, which looked something like they were trying to be amateur anthropologists. She figured it must be an anthropology class.

Immersed in the reading of the course catalog Emily didn't see the numbers ticking up on the gas pump meter. After a few minutes, she heard the pump tick indicating that the tank was full. That was just as John Jr. came strolling out of the gas station. He had a bag of potato chips in his arm, beef sticks, and a rainbowed array of

gummy bears and gummy worms. It was so much food
that he had to cradle it in his arms like a child.

Emily chuckled at the sight of her skinny son carrying
all that food. He was a wiry, rangy boy. She thought that
he looked something like a coyote. He loped as he walked,
bounding on the balls of his feet. It was like he was always
ready to take off running. That was good because he was
headed to school to be a runner. He had the skinny bird
chest of a distance runner, his collarbones jutting out of
his shoulders and his legs were about as skinny as Emily's
herself.

He flopped into the back seat of the car with his arm-
fuls of candy.

Emily smiled. "I wonder where you put it all."

John Jr. shrugged, "I don't put it anywhere. I run it off."

Emily chuckled, "That's probably true."

John Jr. yanked open a bag of gummy bears and
started shoveling them into his mouth by the handful.
John Sr. sat back in the car and let out a groan.

"You better go pro, kid. I'm breaking the bank just
getting you to school."

Through a mouth stuffed with rainbow gummy bears,
John Jr. mumbled, "How far away are we?"

Emily sighed. "Hopefully, we're close to Manners
School."

John Sr. pointed off in the distance. "Those are the
Blue Mountains." John cranks up the car, shifts it into
gear and pulls away from the gas station. "We're about
four hours away."

They pass a sign on the road for the Wild Horse Casino.
The wooden sign looks old and dilapidated. In faded chip-
ping paint, it shows a horse bucking and an arrow.

John points at the sign. "See that? I was reading the

other day that the Wild Horse is actually on the original Oregon Trail."

Emily locks eyes with John Jr. in the rearview mirror and rolls her eyes. "Here he goes again."

John Sr. expressed some mock outrage. "Hey now, this is important stuff. History is important. You know, we're originally Oregonians."

Emily scoffed, "I'm not. I'm 100% Louisiana girl."

It was John Sr.'s chance to roll his eyes. "Fine, except for your mother. She's Cajun and proud. My great grandfather actually went to the University of Oregon. He was a Duck."

John Jr. shoved a handful of sour cream and onion chips in his mouth. Crunching through the chips, he said, "Huh. You never told me that."

John Sr. nodded. "Yep. He was a distance runner, just like you. He actually competed in the Olympics back in 1906. He was a British guy actually, but Oregon had one of the earliest running programs. A year or so before that, he actually traveled around Oregon challenging different people to running contests. He was trying to gin up some excitement for the Olympics. Not a lot of people knew about running as a sport back then."

"How'd he do?" John Jr. asked.

John Sr. smiled into the rearview mirror. "They called him the fastest man in the world back then. He raced all over Oregon and never lost a single race not one. In fact, he even set a world record when he was racing in Walla Walla. It was unofficial but he still did it."

"Wow, that's awesome," John Jr. said. "The fastest man alive."

John Sr. nodded proudly. "Yep. His rifle is even hanging over the bar in some old saloon in Walla Walla. Some people say it was even carried by Lewis and Clark."

Emily exclaimed, "Wow. How'd he get a rifle from Lewis and Clark?"

John Sr. shrugged. "He won it in the race in Walla Walla. They put up a bet, him and the guy he was running against. He won the bet but he didn't want to take something so valuable, so he left it in Walla Walla."

"Who'd he race?" John Jr. asked.

"I don't know. No one really knows. I think it was just some local guy."

John Jr. replied, "Well, that seems kinda unfair. He was a trained runner just racing some random guy."

They merged back onto the interstate and headed down the road. Off to the side of the road, they could see the Wild Horse Casino. Based on the sign, it would have been easy to assume the Wild Horse was going to be a dilapidated shack. Instead, it was actually a pretty sleek operation. The paint looked new and fresh, slathered on in thick crimson layers. The facade was wooden boards. A few of them were askew but they looked to be in decent condition.

John Jr. looked down at the Wild Horse, marveling at the idea of being on the original Oregon Trail. He didn't know much about the Oregon Trail. He'd played the video game when he was a kid in school. Based on that, he assumed dysentery was a pretty big deal back then. Oh, and fording a river was almost always a bad idea but the other options were just as bad. He didn't know much else about it. A bunch of brave settlers had traveled west from what they knew into the great unknown. They found un-inhabited land that was great for farming and free for the taking. That was about all he could remember from school. The Native Americans had moved to reservations and they could open casinos now. Casinos like the Wild Horse.

Down on the service road that fed the Wild Horse

casino, he saw a string of boys. Except for their ruddy reddish brown skin, they could have been John Jr. himself. It was a string of wiry boys with short, dark hair and skinny ankles. They were wearing bright Nike shoes in highlighter colors, split cross country shorts, and sports watches. They were wearing singlets and lightly colored tank tops. There was a boy in the front, though. He was young and skinny. He was shirtless, glistening with sweat. His shorts flapped in the breeze and his bare feet slapped the ground as he ran. His arms and legs pumped in time with each other, moving quickly and swiftly. His head didn't bounce up or down as he ran, his legs moving like pistons.

Unlike the other boys, the boy in the front had long black hair that flowed down his back like a waterfall but was the color of coal. It's unshackled, floating free behind his head, waving in the wind. The boy in the front looked over his shoulder and seemed to lock eyes with John Jr. up on the overpass. They looked at each other for a long while. The young Native boy lifted his hand and waved his acknowledgement at John Jr.

John Jr. waved back.

He turned to his mom and dad. "You guys see his hair? It's awesome."

His mom looked over her shoulder at the line of Native boys running. "Whose hair, honey?"

John Jr. looked back. The boy in the front was no longer there. The line of boys in singlets and running shoes with the short hair are still there, running a quick pace. But the boy in the front with the bare feet and the long hair is gone.

"What?" John Jr. says, baffled. "He was just there."

Emily shrugged. "Maybe he ran off."

John Jr replies, "Maybe."

X

Before

The Liksiyu didn't know where she was or where she was headed. She thought she might be somewhere that hadn't existed before, but it was hard to know for sure. The air was dry and cold, like a tree branch that snapped underfoot. The grass was crisp and brittle, crunching under her feet. The veil of darkness covered the sky with only tiny pinpricks leaking the light of heaven onto the ground. There were more than she could count, but that did not mean she hadn't tried. She was fairly sure she had been a child once. She had memories of childhoods but they could have been anyone's. There were machines she did not understand -- pale faces with eyes the color of shallow water. See saw men with faces the color of redwood trees and eyes like pools of night. These were faces she had never seen before; not their specific features nor their color. They were like the faces of humans from another world. They felt familiar though. They were alien but she might know them. She didn't know how to hold both ideas in her head but there they were. They were like friends she hadn't met yet. Or maybe she had known them forever.

She saw creations of metal -- machines that flew through the sky. She saw towers of glass and steel reaching like pillars into the sky. They were obelisks impossibly tall. What shallow and small tribe had built these? Who was so petty and fragile they needed phalluses of iron to declare their importance?

In some of her thoughts she wasn't herself, but she was. She was a boy -- a boy with long hair down his back, running barefoot through the streets. She could feel her arms and legs pumping in time with her breath. Fire in her chest swelled through her body. There was a white man next to her/him. She didn't know this man, but she felt like she should. They were racing.

She was a scout, creeping through the woods. The ground was wet and hot; soft like the inside of a mouth. The mud squished around her boots as she crept through the steaming woods. She held a weapon in her hands -- a rifle unlike any she'd seen before. The French had brought muskets with them -- they were devastating machines that could end lives. The difference between those and this was the difference between a musket and a spear. This was a black thing -- made of a material she'd never felt before. It was dripping with attachments -- lighter and smaller than a musket but the deadliness was obvious. This was a machine of mass killing.

The Liksiyu felt herself casting about. She was back in her own body, living in her first reality. Was it her first? Did she truly remember her childhood? She could remember being a child in the Northwest -- the arid weather that dried the dirt and swept it across the ground as the wind blew. She remembered running through the mountains with horses on her sides. Her hair flapped in the wind behind her

She remembered another childhood that could not be

the same. She remembered being young and scared. The air was cold and wet. She was standing on the edge of an ocean but not the one from the Northwest. This one was not the calm, placid water. This was roiling and angry and cold. The sun was rising over the edge of the water where it curved into oblivion. The sun was wavering and orange, fighting against the obscurity of a cold haze. She was with other children. The other children were bundled against the cold, watching the horizon. The Liksiyu looked farther out and saw what they were watching -- masts.

There were sails coming over the water, rising like monsters out of the sea. The children watched the boats rise over the horizon with excitement. They jumped and cheered as the boats seem to crawl through the water. There were three of them in all. The children watched them from the rocky shore slippery with wet moss. They made bets about which one would reach the shore first. As they got closer and closer, the children stopped cheering and laughing. They grew quiet, then they started whispering. They'd never seen ships like this before. The children didn't really understand how big the ships would grow as they started over the horizon. Now that they were standing on the cliffs, they could see that they were looking at the sails -- not over the top of them but directly at them. This was something they'd never seen before.

The things that came off the ships were not what they had seen before either. The kids watching had given way to adults standing on the beach. They carried pottery, jewelry, and weapons with them. The pottery and jewelry were going to be for making friends with the newcomers. The weapons were going to be for any failure to make friends. They had assembled the men of the town. They wore their best clothes and accrued their finest ceremonial jewelry. They did not come alone, though. The old men of town -- stooped and hunchbacked from age -- also brought the young men of the town with them. The young men of the town were hard hearted men with the burning fire of youth that often extinguished as a man got older. The young men were men sure of themselves and their skills with a knife.

Nothing prepared them for what came off the ship, though. They waited for men to come from the ship. Men and women with red faces and black hair. They had even been talking among themselves that these might be men and women from across the entire sea. There were rumors of men who came on a ship to the north of these. They had hair that was orange and blonde -- eyes that were green and blue and brown. They were sickly, pale, strange creatures. They carried heavy weapons. That was what the Liksiyu thought she would see getting off this boat whenever it was in time she had drifted. That's not what got off, though. They were not monsters, but they were not men -- not in the usual sense. Instead, they were a singular storm surge. The storm made landfall and instantly began to consume the world. It brought with it hate and panic and fear and anguish. Disease rode on the stormwinds. It smelled like the stinking rot of old death and the hot metallic oozing of new agony. The storm was violent, endless, and greedy. It consumed the world that Liksiyu knew.

Pulled out of the moment, she found herself following the storm through the world. The storm began in the Northeastern art of the continent, by the cold ocean. It swept south into the warmer, soggy parts of the country. The men on horses brought guns and germs and metal. They fired their rifles, ripping the world apart. They spread their illness on purpose and by accident. Their illness was not just physical. They brought boils and bloody saliva and hacking coughs. They brought a pox. The storm carried the devastating wounds that it so mockingly called smallpox.

As it conquered the entire world, shattering families and ripping entire countries apart, the pox didn't feel small. No. It felt very large. Large enough to swallow all of existence. The pox came on the breath, sweat, and blood of the storm. They came as part of it. But they also came on purpose. They were not only part of the fabric of the storm, they were part of the fabric of its blankets. The storm pelted every red face it could with stinging rain and cold. Then, when the body was sufficiently broken, the storm brought blankets and called itself a savior. The blankets weren't salvation though. They were the eye of the storm. After the calm, the destruction bean again.

The Liksiyu watched this unfold with growing horror. She watched the Cherokee forced out of their home by the oncoming storm. She was watching, then, she was one of them. She was in the storm, fleeing from the ravaging squall. She felt the press of bodies all around her -- they were hot and sweating and stinking. They smelled like humanity itself; the savage, bloody simplicity of humanity. You put one foot on the ground, then put another one in front of that one. You trudged forward because you wanted to live. The Liksiyu felt it; it was the strangest feeling. The storm was at her back, pressing like a monster. It lashed her back with driving rain that felt like whips. Looking over her shoulder, she could see the endless swirling darkness behind her. The lightning and thunder was impenetrable; she knew in her heart it would swallow her. It would engulf her and she'd be eviscerated. But still she moved forward, away from the storm. She kept moving her legs because it was a habit. She didn't have much of a hope of ever escaping the storm; she still kept moving forward because that's what humans do. Humans have something that other animals just don't have. Animals might flee from danger because they're afraid; humans can do that too. That's true. However, they also might run because they think they can escape. It's not instinct that makes humans run. It's the hope that they can get free; it's the humanity. That's what the storm takes.

If hope makes somebody human, then the storm makes people less than human. It steals the hope from people. That's how you can steal someone's land and their lives. If they have hope, they'll never give up. But if you can take their hope, you can drive them at the edge of the storm. That's what the storm does.

The Liksiyu keeps running from the storm. While she's running from the storm that presses at her back, the clouds and thunder devouring the ground, she finds herself back in the Northwest. She's been pushed to the extreme edge of the country. At her back is the storm, and in front of her is the cold ocean. She keeps running. Running straight for the ocean. She found she wasn't alone, though.

Rushing away from the storm that was consuming the entire world, she found someone ahead of her. She saw a person she'd been. Or a person she had thought she was. She saw the long-haired man with the bare feet and the strong legs. She knew him. She could feel the fire burning in his chest. She could feel the acid burning in the muscles in his legs. She knew this man, this Cayuse.

This was the last of the Cayuse. The Liksiyu could feel the link between herself and the Cayuse boy ahead of her. He was slender and muscular. His back was muscled and strong -- like a bag of ropes underneath her skin. She tried to get closer to him, but he was always ahead of her.

She knew his name. She heard the wind whispering his name. It whispered the name of the thin man with the strong back and the rippling muscles in his legs. She heard his name from the wind; the storm screamed and raged at him.

Blackie, it said. *You'll never escape the storm, Blackie.*

The Liksiyu saw the fire ahead of her. The fire that had started all of this. It had gone out so long ago. She didn't know when or where she'd been when that had happened. Had she ever been alive? Had she imagined the fire? Had she imagined the fire that raged and flickered then went quiet? She'd placed her hand in the ashes of the fire but found they were cold. Cold as if they had never even been lit. The fire had been lit, though. She knew the fire had been lit. That fire had been the Liksiyu's. It had been her people.

She knew she hadn't imagined the fire. In fact, the fire hadn't even gone out. She saw it up ahead of her. She saw it bouncing through the clouds. It was smaller and dimmer, but it didn't die. It was bobbing on the top of a torch. The torch was the hefty branch of a redwood tree wrapped with a rag soaked in oil. The fire flickered but refused to die. Blackie was carrying it. He was carrying the fire from the Liksiyu.

The future of the Cayuse was carried through Blackie Sullivan. His name lived on even though he surrendered back to the earth. There are few people who know the truth about the man who lived in Walla Walla. They know about Natives who beat white invaders on the battlefield; they know even more who were killed by the churning, gnashing thresher that was Manifest Destiny.

That's what they called it. The presidents of the United States, they were all different but most felt the same, determined that it was their destiny. They believed that God himself had granted them an entire continent that would stretch from the East to the West. It was not lost on the Native Americans that the Good Lord has only seen fit to promise land to white people. And only land that wasn't already occupied by powerful white governments. They could have stretched north into Canada, but that was apparently not what the Lord had set aside for them. They did stretch south though. They plundered, raped, and pillaged Mexico from the Mexicans. They only stopped when they grew tired.

The storm that Liksiyu witnessed had slowed to a trickle by the time Blackie Sullivan was a man. It had devoured nearly every Native American who had once dotted the land. They'd lived for thousands of years -- they fought, stole, and pillaged. The Natives were human -- not perfect. Some tribes disappeared because of feast, famine, and war. But the Native Americans survived. They survived the storm too -- the storm that was white people. They didn't survive without mass casualties though. What they lost was measured in lives and wealth. The amount of blood shed by Native Americans as the storm raged would be enough to fill an ocean. It would be enough to water the entire continent and grow an empire.

They survived though, because they kept moving their feet forward and hoping for a better future. Blackie was one of those people. He was the last Cayuse and one of the last natives. They would keep on; they always did. But they would continue forward in a diminished way. Those who had lived through the storm were stronger for the experience, but they should never have had to go through it.

Maybe that's what led John Jr. into the woods that day. He didn't know. They had been in Walla Walla for a cross country meet. The Whitman Blues weren't the most talented or well-funded group. They definitely weren't the kind of school that normally participate in meets against the Oregon Ducks. They had a lovely route through the Blue Mountains, though. That had led some nearby schools to compete in the mountains outside Walla Walla. The high altitude, the dry air, and the steep climbs were a great way to train for bigger meets.

John Jr., panting and heaving in the dry air, felt the training working. If you had asked him at that moment, he would have said he didn't feel it was that great of a workout. It might be effective, but it didn't seem great. He walked through the woods, trying to catch his breath. Many of the upperclassmen had kept running the route -- the team would be in Walla Walla for a few more days. John Jr. wasn't prepared for this, though. He couldn't keep up with the juniors and seniors who had been keeping up this brutal pace for years. So, he walked slowly through the woods as the sun beamed through the leaves and dappled the ground.

As he walked, a breeze cut through the trees and pushed the leaves aside. There, down a small, overgrown trail was a cabin. The cabin was tiny and dilapidated. The boards were falling and rotting. There were gaps where the boards had fallen to the ground or been scavenged for firewood. The porch had collapsed decades ago, it seemed. Now there was just a house with holes in the roof and a tiny stream running next to the cabin.

He didn't know why, but John Jr. decided to walk down the path he'd found. He picked his way through the brush and trees. He pushed away branches and slipped under twisting vines. It was only a few feet. He tiptoed through the woods into the clearing with the cabin. The summer had been unseasonably hot and dry, so the grass was not as high as it could be. It was up to John Jr's ankles, dry and crackling underfoot. He walked up to the cabin and heard skittering and scratching from the dark interior in the cabin. He didn't know what the creature was, but there was something in there. Something was alive. He decided to steer clear. Instead, he spotted a stump sitting by the creek.

He walked over and sat on the stump, watching the water trickle slowly. The water was cool and crystal blue. It had to be fed by mountain snowmelt. Water moving that slowly had no business being as clear as it was. It had to be fresh and untouched by man. Americans had a way of ruining things that were good and simple. They hated quiet.

That's what John Jr, found here. He found quiet. He sat on the stump, catching his breath. He listened to the babbling of the creek and felt himself growing calmer. His heartbeat slowed and his mind cleared. The water was clear and soft. The sun peeked from behind a few clouds and hit the water. The softness disappeared; it was replaced by the light dancing off the tiny peaks and valleys of the water. Each inch of the water glittered like a diamond, and then like a star, it twinkled out of existence. But there was another shimmering in the bottom of the brook. He looked down at the water and saw that there was something buried in the silt. He got to his hands and knees and crawled to the edge of the water so he could peer in. There below the surface something shimmered; it looked like metal.

John Jr. reached down into the water. It was colder than he'd imagined; it had to be snow runoff. The water climbed up to his shoulder before he got to the bottom of the creek. He grabbed a handful of the silty creek floor until he grabbed hold of the metal object. He pulled his hand up, letting the silt drain away as the water pulled it back into the creek. He opened his hand to find something he didn't quite understand. It was a metal ball, perfectly smooth. It was about the size of a marble but made of metal. It was a dull yellow color. He rubbed it on his running shorts a few times, and it buffed like the metal of a car. It shimmered where he'd rubbed it against his pants, shining like a light.

Is this gold? It definitely looked like gold but it was a perfect ball. If he was being honest with himself, it looked like a Civil War musket ball. A golden musket ball. Who would make a musket ball out of solid gold? In high school, John Jr. had read in a textbook that Civil War soldiers used any metal they could find to make musket balls. The Civil War had never gotten all the way to Washington, though. This was definitely odd.

He didn't have long to ponder it, though. The light shifted, and he saw another glinting metal in the water. Was this another yellow musket ball? He looked closer, crawling back to the edge of the water to look. No, not a musket ball. This one was much duller and grimier. He plunged his hand back into the cool water to investigate. His hand found the cold metal but he couldn't grab it. He fished around for it until he finally got his fingers around it. It was bigger than he thought. He pulled at it. It didn't budge. He pulled again and it broke free of the muddy creek bottom. It wasn't some small piece of metal. The ground lifted up in a massive heap. The mud slipped away. He was holding a rifle.

It was a decrepit thing that looked older even than the muskets he'd seen in pictures of the Civil War. It was as long as John Jr. was tall. It was covered in mud and grime. Algae was growing down the barrel and the wooden stock was slick with rot. The wooden stock was worn smooth by however long it had been in the water. The entire metal barrel was coated in a thick layer of rust.

John Jr. got to his feet so he could better inspect the rifle. The stock had a metal inlay. It might have been gold once but now it was just completely brown. It was speckled with flecks of white corrosion. John Jr. Rubbed at it with his shorts; the grime wasn't coming off though. The years in the mud were too much for him to buff out with his shorts. He couldn't undo the damage time had done.

He looked at the engraving in the metal inlay, though. It looked like some people on a horse. They were packed for an expedition of some sort. He rubbed the stock; there was an engraving too. It was a little bit sloppier; it looked like it had been put into the stock by hand. Someone with a steady hand but still someone with a knife in hand. The words were faded and worn smooth by the years of running water wearing away at the edges of the letters.

John Jr could just barely make out the words: If found, return to Blackie Sullivan.

John Jr. thought that was odd. He'd never even heard of anyone named Blackie Sullivan.

To no one in particular, he wondered aloud, "Who was Blackie Sullivan?"

Epilogue

The stories that have been told about Blackie Sullivan weren't the only stories of the Cayuse or of Walla Walla. They aren't the only stories of the people who were in the country before the storm. They did not call the country one country in those days. The Lakota called it Lakota. The Apache called it Apache Country. They were hundreds of countries, destined to be smashed against the rocks or be swallowed by the coming storm. But they did not disappear; just because you cannot always see them does not mean they disappeared. In hushed tones and after sideways glances over their shoulders, they told stories. There are those who say that Blackie Sullivan did not ever go away either. They say he ran and he ran but he never stopped.

The Copper Canyons of northern Mexico are as far from Walla Walla as somewhere can be on the same continent. The bitter cold that grips Walla Walla during the winter when the sun goes down and plunges the West into darkness does not touch the Copper Canyons. The air in Walla Walla, so dry the sweat never has time to collect and the vessels in your nose sometimes shrink until they rupture are no issue in the Canyons. There, the heat rises up from underneath you in the form of steam and soggy wet air. The air is thick with humidity to the point that breathing feels like a mouth full of wet rags. No one could run in those mountains, many would say.

The ground is too soft and muddy. The heat is too high, and the air too thin. At that elevation, it's a wonder air that threadbare can even hold the water it does, but it does. And someone can. Someone can run in those mountains, dodging pebbles, rattlesnakes, fallen trees, and an approaching storm. Blackie could. Some say Blackie did. They say they saw Blackie in the Copper Canyons of Mexico.

He walked barefoot into the Canyons with the mud squelching between his toes. What he found -- if indeed he go on foot and not only in spirit -- were a people who had faced the storm. They'd weathered the pelting rain and pounding hail to arrive intact but battered. They had been blown by the winds far from where they had begun but there is no destination for them, only the journey. If the meeting ever did happen, guided by the Liksiyu, Blackie Sullivan tiptoed slowly to a clearing in the woods.

A woman emerged, wrapped in a wool blanket spun from the rough fibers of mountain goats. It was hardy and warm but scratchy. She had it draped around her shoulders and a hat pulled lower over her eyes. The sun was high and hot but her hat cast a shadow over her eyes. She lifted a hand and spoke to him.

"Hello," she said. "Have you finally come at last?" If this happened, Blackie would have understood her. He would have understood her words maybe, but he definitely would have understood the desperate plea. The storm had dragged men and women, girls and boys, from their beds to work in mines. The storm called it progress.

In the slippery, hot mud of the land, Blackie would have listened to her speak about the storm. She would have told him that her home is called the Copper Canyons because of the metal that was found there. The metal had to be pulled out of the earth by carving deep jagged wounds into the earth and disemboweling its innards. The guts of the world, shimmering in their copper brilliance were worth money to the Spaniards. So, they enslaved her people and forced them to work. The people are not clear if it was Liksiyu who taught them how to survive or if Blackie did. Maybe Blackie was drawn to them just because they were touched by the same spirit. Whatever the truth might be, those people called themselves the Raramuri. In their language, it means "the people who run." They maybe never met Blackie, but they all ran just the same.

There are those in the north who lived on land that was more ice than dirt. They called themselves by many different names. But they wore cloaks with the fur turned inward and sealskin to keep the water off them. They were a people who grew hardy and low to the ground, their bodies uniquely designed for the frozen hills. Blackie, with his slender hips and narrow shoulders, would not have fit in among those people physically. But they welcomed him none the same, if he ever went there. They told stories about the boy who ran and never stopped. He had no boat that would get him from Washington to Alaska or to the snowy reaches of Canada. Surely, he could not have run across the ocean. Could he? If you ask the people who call the knee-deep snow home, they will say it is possible.

They aren't known for running. There's not far for them to go. But they rowed their sealskin boats with the commitment and tenacity that pushed Blackie. If he had ever gone there, he would have felt at home among the sled dogs. They ran and ran and never stopped.

Maybe Blackie just bred horses for the rest of his life. He'd learned about breeding and training horses from his father and some of the other Cayuse men. They were the men who could tuck a wad of sagebrush in their cheek to freshen up their tobacco and spit into the dirt with rifle accuracy. They would stand and watch the horses mill around in the field. After a few spits into the dirt and watching the horses canter around in the field, they could decide which ones were ready to race and which ones were workhorses. There was no breaking of horses in the traditional sense. A horse didn't need to be broken, it needed to be freed. If a horse trusted you, it would let you ride. So, maybe that's what Blackie had done. Maybe Blackie had spent his time with these creatures that were also born to run.

Blackie's father was the last Cayuse. Blackie was only half a Cayuse but his heart was completely Cayuse. His horse training skills were completely Cayuse. Everything about him was rooted in the dirt and the earth where he had grown up. His bare feet were indistinguishable from the hooves of the horses kicking up dust.

═══════════════

No one knows what happened to Blackie when he ran ahead of the storm. He had disappeared from the history books. There were many different tribes and nations that had stories of Blackie or someone who could be Blackie. There, in the woods outside Walla Walla, a horse walked slowly through the woods. There was no saddle on its back and no bit in its mouth. Its ears perked up when the wind shifted.

Somewhere, riding on the wind, a boy holding a rifle asked "Who is Blackie Sullivan?"

Blackie, hearing his name on the wind, responded. "I'm Blackie Sullivan. I'm still here."

Printed in the United States
By Bookmasters